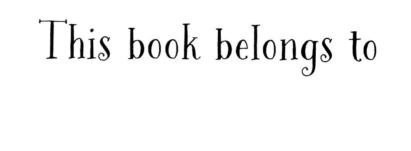

This book belongs to

..............................................................................

# Illustrated Treasury of
# Classic
# Stories

First published in 2015 by Miles Kelly Publishing Ltd
Harding's Barn, Bardfield End Green, Thaxted, Essex, CM6 3PX, UK

Copyright © Miles Kelly Publishing Ltd 2015

This edition published 2016

2 4 6 8 10 9 7 5 3 1

Publishing Director Belinda Gallagher
Creative Director Jo Cowan
Editorial Director Rosie Neave
Design Manager Joe Jones
Cover Designer Jo Cowan
Production Elizabeth Collins, Caroline Kelly
Reprographics Stephan Davis, Jennifer Cozens, Thom Allaway
Assets Lorraine King

ISBN 978-1-78617-097-2

Printed in China

British Library Cataloguing-in-Publication Data
A catalogue record for this book is available from the British Library

## ACKNOWLEDGMENTS

The publishers would like to thank the following artists
who have contributed to this book:
Cover: Marcela Calderón
Inside pages: Cosei Kawa (Advocate Art), Jan Lewis, Ayesha Lopez (Advocate Art),
Kristina Swarner (The Bright Agency), Milena Jahier, Laura Wood

Made with paper from a sustainable forest

**www.mileskelly.net**

# CONTENTS

# NEW FRIENDS

# SECRETS REVEALED

# SAVING THE DAY

# MUCH MISCHIEF

# ABOUT THE AUTHORS

Learn more about some of the famous
authors behind these much-loved stories.

## Louisa May Alcott
## 1832-1888

*Little Women* is Alcott's most famous book. She
began it in the hope it might pay off some of her
family's debts. In it, she told stories from her
own childhood with her sisters May, Elizabeth,
and Anna. It was an enormous success and she
became both wealthy and an unwilling celebrity.

"Christmas Wishes" from *Little Women*

## Anna Sewell
## 1820-1878

Lamed in an accident when she was fourteen,
Sewell often traveled by carriage, and hated the
cruel treatment of the horses. She wrote *Black
Beauty* in response to this, saying its special
aim was "to induce sympathy, kindness, and an
understanding treatment of horses."

"Ginger" and "A Stormy Day" from *Black Beauty*

# About the Authors

## Lewis Carroll
## 1832-1898

Carroll spent his adult life at Oxford University in the UK, teaching and studying mathematics and logic. He invented the story that would later become *Alice's Adventures in Wonderland* while out on a boat trip with the three daughters of a friend—Lorina, Edith, and Alice Liddell.

"Down the Rabbit-hole" and "A Mad Tea-party" from *Alice's Adventures in Wonderland* • "Wool and Water" from *Through the Looking-glass*

## Frances Hodgson Burnett
## 1849-1924

Burnett's childhood was one of poverty—an experience that she would later include in some of her novels. In 1865 her family moved from Manchester in England to Tennessee in the United States, where she began to earn money writing for magazines. She went on to write more than forty books.

"Sara" and "A French Lesson" from *A Little Princess* • "The Key to the Garden" and "The Robin who Showed the Way" from *The Secret Garden*

## L. Frank Baum
### 1856-1919

Lyman Frank Baum hated his first name and preferred to be called Frank. His greatest success was *The Wonderful Wizard of Oz*, and he went on to write thirteen books about the magical land of Oz, and many other short stories, poems and scripts.

"The Journey Begins" from *The Wonderful Wizard of Oz*

## Susan Coolidge
### 1835-1905

Coolidge was interested in writing from a young age, and turned to it as a career after working as a nurse during the American Civil War. Her own family—Susan herself, her three younger sisters, her brother, and her cousin—were the inspiration for the Carr family in *What Katy Did*, and the four books in the series that followed.

"The Little Carrs" from *What Katy Did*

# About the Authors

## Kenneth Grahame
### 1859-1932

Grahame's mother died when he was five, and he and his siblings were raised by their grandmother. Unable to afford to go to university, he took a job in the Bank of England. Grahame began to write about the characters that would later appear in *The Wind in the Willows* in letters to his son.

"The Riverbank" and "The Wild Wood" from *The Wind in the Willows*

## E. Nesbit
### 1858-1924

Nesbit used the initial "E" rather than her full name, "Edith," to disguise the fact that she was a woman. She wrote more than forty books for children, and created the idea of mixing real-life characters and settings with magical elements.

"The Terrible Secret" and "Saviors of the Train" from *The Railway Children*
"Golden Guineas" from *Five Children and It*

# ABOUT THE ARTISTS

***Milena Jahier*** Born in Argentina, Milena grew up in England and Mexico before moving to Italy to study illustration at the European Institute of Design. Since then she has worked on designs for packaging, products, and logos, as well as illustrating greeting cards, murals, and books. She works traditionally, using mixed media on paper.
*Sara • A French Lesson*

***Cosei Kawa*** Since finishing his MA in Illustration at University College Falmouth in the UK, Cosei has illustrated numerous children's books. He uses a variety of mediums including acrylic, watercolor, collage, and digital effects to create work that is both naïve and detailed. He lives in Kyoto, Japan where he also teaches illustration at Kyoto University of Art and Design, and enjoys meditation, reading and music.
*The Key to the Garden • The Robin Who Showed the Way*

***Jan Lewis*** Based in Oxfordshire in the UK, Jan has been working as an illustrator since 1978. She has produced work for many publishers, as well as BBC children's television. Since gaining her MA in Authorial Illustration Jan has enjoyed writing and illustrating her own books for children.
*The Riverbank • The Wild Wood • A Mad Tea-party • Wool and Water*

# About the Artists

***Ayesha Lopez*** As a small child, Ayesha loved to draw—unluckily for her parents, this meant drawing on their furniture. Now she combines paper and computer to produce her charming, quirky illustrations. She lives in London, UK.
*The Caravan Siege • Two Visits and What Came of Them • Christmas Wishes*

***Kristina Swarner*** Magical and dreamlike, Kristina's work draws much of its imagery and inspiration from memories of exploring old houses, woods, and gardens when she was a child. She lives in Chicago, U.S., where she illustrates all kinds of things from books, greeting cards, and magazines to wine labels and theater posters.
*Ginger • A Stormy Day • Pollyanna and Punishments • The Little Carrs • The Banquet Lamp*

***Laura Wood*** Growing up in the north of Italy, Laura devoured books and drew on the kitchen walls of her parents' house. She is now a full-time illustrator of picture books, educational publications, and digital apps, among other things. She lives between Bristol, Melbourne, and Milan, and she especially loves the process of finding the right color palette, and bumping into funny (and furry!) characters in amusing stories.
*The Journey Begins • The Terrible Secret • Saviors of the Train • Golden Guineas*

# ALONE IN THE WORLD

# Sara

From *A Little Princess*
by Frances Hodgson Burnett

Once on a dark winter's day, when the yellow fog hung so thick and heavy in the streets of London that the lamps were lighted and the shop windows blazed with gas as they do at night, a little girl sat in a cab with her father and was driven rather slowly through the big thoroughfares.

She sat with her feet tucked under her, leaning against her father, who held her in the crook of his arm as she stared out of the window at the passing people with a thoughtfulness in her big eyes.

"Papa," she said in a low, mysterious little voice which was almost a whisper, "papa."

"What is it, darling?" Captain Crewe answered, holding her closer and looking down into her face.

"Is this the place?" Sara whispered, cuddling still closer to him. "Is it, papa?"

"Yes, little Sara, it is. We have reached it at last."

And though she was only seven years old, she knew that he felt sad when he said it. It seemed to her many years since he had begun to prepare her mind for "the place," as she always called it. Her mother had died when she was born. Her young, handsome, rich, doting father seemed to be the only relation she had in the world. She only knew he was rich because she had heard people say so. She had always lived in a beautiful bungalow, and had been used to seeing many servants who let her have her own way in everything. She had learned that people who were rich had these things.

During her short life only one thing had

troubled her, and that thing was the "place" she was to be taken to some day. She had seen other children go away to school, and had known that she would be obliged to go also, and she had been troubled by the thought that her father could not stay with her.

"Couldn't you go to that place with me, papa?" she had asked when she was five years old. "I would help you with your lessons."

"But you will not have to stay for long, Sara," he always said. "There will be a lot of little girls, and you will play together, and you will grow so fast that it will seem scarcely a year before you are big and clever enough to come back and take care of papa."

"Well, papa" she said softly, "if we are here I suppose we must be resigned."

He laughed at her old-fashioned speech and kissed her. He was not resigned himself, though he knew he must keep that a secret. His little Sara had been a great companion to him, and he felt he should be lonely when, on his return to India, he went into his house knowing he need not expect to see the small figure come to meet him. So he held her in his arms as the cab rolled into the square in which stood the house which was their destination.

It was a big, dull, brick house, and when they got close to the door they could see there shone a brass plate on which was engraved in black letters:

MISS MINCHIN,
SELECT SEMINARY FOR YOUNG LADIES

"Here we are, Sara," said Captain Crewe, making his voice sound as cheerful as possible. Sara often thought afterward that the house was somehow exactly like Miss Minchin. It was respectable and well furnished, but everything in it was ugly. The drawing room into which they were ushered was covered by a carpet with a square pattern upon it, the chairs were square, and a heavy marble timepiece stood upon the heavy marble mantel.

As she sat down in one of the chairs, Sara cast one of her quick looks about her. "I don't like it, papa," she said. "But then I dare say soldiers—even brave ones—don't really like going into battle."

Captain Crewe laughed outright at this. He never tired of hearing Sara's queer speeches. "Oh, little Sara," he said. "What shall I do when I have no one to say solemn things to me?" And then suddenly he swept her into his arms and kissed her, looking almost as if tears had come into his eyes.

It was just then that Miss Minchin entered the room. She had large, cold, fishy eyes, and a large, cold, fishy smile. It spread itself into a very large smile when she saw Sara and Captain Crewe. She had heard a great many desirable things of the young soldier from the lady who had recommended her school to him. Among other things, she had heard that he was a rich father who was willing to spend a great deal of money on his little daughter.

"It will be a great privilege to have charge of such a beautiful, promising child, Captain Crewe," she said, taking Sara's hand. "Lady Meredith has told me of her cleverness. A clever child is a great treasure in an establishment like mine."

Sara stood quietly, with her eyes fixed upon Miss Minchin's face. "Why does she say I am a beautiful child?" she was thinking. "I am not beautiful at all. Colonel Grange's little girl, Isobel, is beautiful. She has dimples and rose-colored cheeks, and long hair the color of gold. I have black hair and green eyes; besides which, I am a thin child and not fair in the least. I am one of the ugliest children I ever saw. She is beginning by telling a story."

She was mistaken, however, in thinking she was

an ugly child. She was not in the least like Isobel Grange, who had been the beauty of the regiment, but she had an odd charm of her own. She was a slim, supple creature, rather tall for her age, and had an intense, attractive little face. Her hair was heavy and quite black and only curled at the tips; her eyes were greenish gray, it is true, but they were big, wonderful eyes with long, black lashes, and though she herself did not like the color of them, many other people did. Still she was very firm in her belief that she was an ugly little girl, and she was not at all elated by Miss Minchin's flattery.

After she had known Miss Minchin longer she learned that she said the same thing to each papa and mamma who brought a child to her school.

Sara stood near her father and listened while he and Miss Minchin talked. She had been brought to the seminary because Lady Meredith's two little girls had been educated there, and Captain Crewe had a great respect for Lady Meredith's experience.

Sara was to be what was known as a "parlor boarder," and she was to enjoy greater privileges than parlor boarders usually did. She was to have a bedroom and sitting room of her own; she was to have a pony and a carriage, and a maid to take the place of the ayah who had been her nurse in India.

"I am not in the least anxious about her education," Captain Crewe said with a light laugh, as he held Sara's hand and patted it. "She is always sitting with her little nose burrowing into books, and she wants grown-up books—great, big, fat ones—French and German as well as English— history and biography and poets, and all sorts of things. Drag her away from her books when she reads too much. Make her ride her pony or go out and buy a new doll. She ought to play more with dolls."

"Papa," said Sara, "if I went out and bought a new doll every day I should have more than I could be fond of. Emily is going to be my best friend."

Captain Crewe looked at Miss Minchin and Miss Minchin looked at Captain Crewe.

"Who is Emily?" she inquired.

Sara's green-gray eyes looked very solemn and quite soft as she answered.

"She is a doll I haven't got yet," she said. "We are going out together to find her. I have called her Emily. She is going to be my friend when papa is gone. I want her to talk to about him."

Miss Minchin's fishy smile became very flattering indeed. "What an original child!" she said.

"Yes," said Captain Crewe, drawing Sara close. "She is a darling little creature. Take great care of her for me, Miss Minchin."

Sara stayed with her father at his hotel until he sailed away again to India. They went out and visited many shops together, and bought a great many things. They bought, indeed, a great many more things than Sara needed, but Captain Crewe wanted his little girl to have everything she admired and everything he admired himself, so between them they collected a wardrobe much too grand for a child of seven. There were velvet dresses, and lace dresses, and embroidered ones, and hats with great ostrich feathers, and ermine coats, and boxes of gloves and handkerchiefs and silk stockings in such abundant supplies that the polite young women behind the counters whispered to each other that the little girl must be at least some foreign princess.

And at last they found Emily, but they went to a number of toy shops and looked at a great many dolls before they discovered her.

"I want her to look as if she wasn't a doll really," Sara said. "I want her to look as if she listens when I talk to her." So they looked at big ones and little ones, at dolls with black eyes and dolls with blue, at dolls with brown curls and dolls with golden braids.

After a number of disappointments they decided to walk and look in at the shop windows and let the cab follow them. They had passed two or three places without even going in, when, as they were approaching a shop which was really not a very large one, Sara suddenly clutched her father's arm. "Oh, papa!" she cried. "There is Emily!"

A flush had risen to her face and there was an expression in her green-gray eyes as if she had just recognized someone she was fond of.

"She is actually waiting there for us!" she said. "Let us go in to her."

"Dear me," said Captain Crewe, "I feel as if we ought to have someone to introduce us."

"You must introduce me and I will introduce you," said Sara. "I knew her the minute I saw her."

She had certainly a very intelligent expression in her eyes when Sara took her in her arms. She was a large doll, but not too large to carry about easily. She had naturally curling golden-brown hair, and her eyes were a deep, gray-blue, with thick eyelashes that were real eyelashes and not mere painted lines.

"Of course," said Sara, looking into her face as

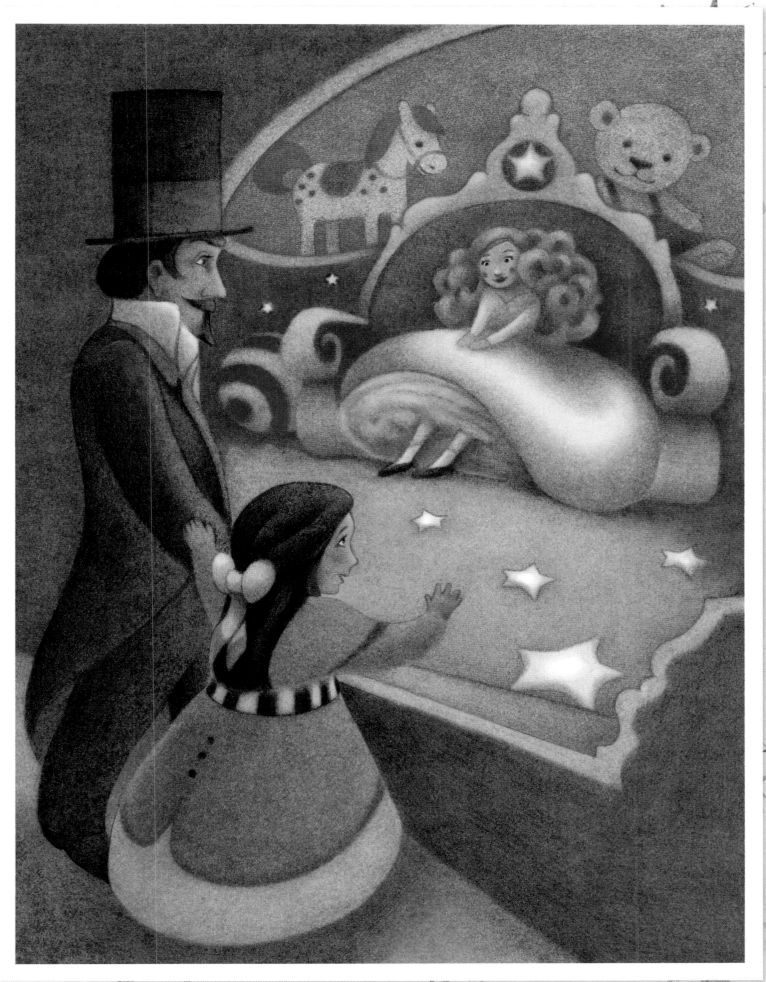

she held her on her knee, "papa, this is Emily."

So Emily was bought and actually taken to a children's outfitter's shop and measured for a wardrobe as grand as Sara's own. She had lace frocks, too, and velvet and muslin ones, and hats and coats and beautiful lace-trimmed underclothes, as well as gloves and handkerchiefs and furs.

"I should like her to look as if she was a child with a good mother," said Sara. "I'm her mother, though I am going to make a companion of her."

Captain Crewe would really have enjoyed the shopping tremendously, but that a sad thought kept tugging at his heart. This all meant that he was going to be parted from his beloved little comrade.

He got out of his bed in the middle of that night and went and stood looking down at Sara, who lay asleep with Emily in her arms. Her black hair was spread out on the pillow and Emily's golden-brown hair mingled with it, both of them had lace-ruffled nightgowns, and both had long eyelashes which lay up on their cheeks. Emily looked so like a real child that Captain Crewe felt glad she was there.

"Heigh-ho, little Sara!" he said to himself. "You don't know how much your daddy will miss you."

The next day he took her to Miss Minchin's. He was to sail the next morning. He explained to Miss Minchin that his solicitors had charge of his affairs in England and would give her any advice she wanted, and that they would pay the bills she sent for Sara's expenses. He would write to Sara twice a week, and she was to be given every pleasure she asked for. "She is a sensible little thing, and never wants anything it isn't safe to give her," he said.

Then he went with Sara into her little sitting room and they bade each other goodbye. Sara sat on his knee and held the lapels of his coat in her small hands, and looked long and hard at his face.

"Are you learning me by heart, little Sara?" he said, stroking her hair.

"No," she answered. "I know you by heart. You

are inside my heart." And they hugged as if they would never let each other go.

When the cab drove away from the door, Sara was sitting on the floor of her sitting room, with her hands under her chin and her eyes following it until it had turned the corner of the square. Emily was sitting by her. When Miss Minchin sent her sister, Miss Amelia, to see what the child was doing, she found she could not open the door.

"I have locked it," said a queer, polite little voice from inside. "I want to be quite by myself, please."

Miss Amelia was fat and dumpy, and much in awe of her sister. She was the better-natured person of the two, but she never disobeyed Miss Minchin. She went downstairs again, looking almost alarmed.

"I never saw such a funny, old-fashioned child, sister," she said. "She has locked herself in, and she is not making the least particle of noise."

"It is much better than if she screamed, as some of them do," Miss Minchin answered. "I expected that a child as much spoiled as she is would set the whole house in an uproar. If ever a child was given her own way in everything, she is."

"I've been putting her things away," said Miss Amelia. "I never saw anything like them—sable and ermine on her coats, and beautiful lace on her underclothing. You have seen some of her clothes. What do you think of them?"

"I think they are perfectly ridiculous," replied Miss Minchin, sharply; "but they will look very well at the head of the line when we take the schoolchildren to church on Sunday. She has been provided for as if she were a little princess."

And upstairs in the locked room Sara and Emily sat on the floor and stared at the corner around which the cab had disappeared, while Captain Crewe looked backward, waving and kissing his hand as if he could not bear to stop.

# The Caravan Siege

by Alice Massie

The door of the country school was open, and the gray-green hills could peep in, and see the children came from prosperous farms—for the valley was a rich one. The children of farm laborers went chiefly to the school at the other end of the valley. No one could say why the children were divided up like this, but the fact remained that the only badly dressed and hungry-looking child in the south school was Tom Darrington, and he was lame, so that he could not be expected to tramp up to the north end of the valley as his sisters and brothers had done.

Tom was rather a pet in the school. The girls from Croft Farm shared their lunch with him. They were twins, and rode in on ponies, which they put up in stables at the back of the school.

Miss Bolt, the school mistress, with her eyes upon the lovely view, said: "I think you could sing your fairy chorus with great expression on a day like this. Trebles, take one long look at the beautiful hills before you start, and then fix your eyes on me." The voices lifted very prettily:

*Fairy folk, fairy folk, down from the mountains,*
*Pitter pat—fairy feet ringing along.*
*Pitter pat—pitter pat—like fairy fountains—*
*Why do you hurry, still singing your song?*

"Now, Ida."
Ida blushed and coughed, and began the solo

part awkwardly, but her voice was full, and rich, and rather mournful:

*People of earth, we have lost a fair daughter,*
*Say have you seen her—oh say if you can—*

Ida stopped short half-way through her solo; there was a sudden movement through the class. Miss Bolt turned toward the door at the side. Leaning against the doorframe was a slender, graceful girl. She wore shoes but no stockings, and a shabby cotton frock. Her hair stood out like an aureole, and the sun shone through it.

Tommy Darrington said out loud, not knowing that he had spoke: "It's the fairy daughter!"

Miss Bolt said: "What is it, dear?" The girl stepped into the room and came to Miss Bolt's desk. The whole school watched her.

"Oh if you please," said the girl, "I want to come to school. We've just moved into the valley, and Father thought I'd better come."

The whole school gasped. No one had moved into the valley. Was Tommy right—was this a fairy? The Croft Farm girls believed she might be; she was very pretty.

Miss Bolt said: "Ida, take my book and make the class repeat the words of the other verses—they don't know them properly." And she led the newcomer out into the sunshine.

When Miss Bolt came in again every eye was fixed upon her. She smiled, and said: "Tomorrow we shall have a new schoolfellow. Her name is Olga Gray. Now we will go on with the singing."

The next morning, Olga came to school early. She was very pretty, eager to make friends, and bright at lessons. At lunchtime all the girls hung round her.

Ella Croft said: "Where do you live, Olga?"

Olga replied: "In London, but we're staying here while Daddy's ill."

"She lives—" said Ida, and then stopped.

"Then you're in lodgings?" said Ella. That explained it. One of the farmers had taken them.

"Sort of," said Olga, smiling.

"Sort of!" repeated Ida. Ida, with her lovely voice, had been the unofficial head of the school; she could see at once that this pretty new girl, who could sing nearly as well as she could herself, would be their queen at once.

"She doesn't live anywhere," said Betty Croft. "She's the fairy down from the hills."

Ida sniffed.

When school was over, the Croft girls wanted to ride up the valley with Olga, but she said: "Daddy will come down to meet me, and he can't bear strangers—not till he's stronger if you don't mind."

So the Croft girls watched her running up the track beside the silver birches, looking more than ever like a fairy. When she had passed out of sight, Ida Burman spoke. "I tell you why she won't let you go with her; she's a gypsy; she lives in a caravan!"

Ella and Betty Croft looked at each other, and they laughed. "A gypsy!" said Betty. "With fair hair like that and speaking as she does! You're only jealous, Ida, because she's prettier than you."

"If you had said she was a fairy now—" said Ella.

"I tell you," said Ida, "they came down that track two days ago. My uncle wouldn't let them camp on his land—he didn't want his chickens stolen. Mr. Graham let them have his little spinney place."

Ella started her pony. "They're certainly not gypsies," she said.

"They are!" said Ida. "You'll have Olga selling clothes pegs at your door, you see! A girl like that ought not to come to our school."

"Rubbish!" said Betty. But all the same she stopped in the middle of a game of tennis that evening to stare at a pedlar woman who was going to the back door with a basket. Was she possibly a relative of Olga Gray's?

At school Olga was very reticent. Her mother was dead, she and her father lived together and a "man" of father's cooked for them and looked after them. That startled the school. What sort of man? Rumors floated about of a strange, bent man seen in Mr. Graham's spinney, where the van was. Someone said they had seen the van, but was hardly believed, because to get to Mr. Graham's spinney you had to go practically across his lawn, and Mr. Graham was touchy about his land and trespassers.

On the June 23rd the school was reading part of Shakespeare's *A Midsummer Night's Dream*, and Tommy Darrington put up his hand.

"Please, teacher," he said, "I seen a fairy dance."

"Have you, Tommy? Where?"

"Back of Mr. Graham's house, miss, please. And there was lovely fairy music."

"How delightful! Well, as this is Midsummer Eve now, you'd better look out again tonight."

Betty Croft was watching Olga. She saw Olga half turn to Tommy with a startled look in her eye, and a soft flush mounted to her face.

"I believe she is a fairy—really I believe she is," thought Betty.

Ida Burman put her hand on Betty's rein at close of school, and said, "Doris, and Hetty, and Bill Smith, and myself, and one or two more, we're going up to that caravan tonight—to find out things. We can sneak up between the haycocks and no one will see us. Like to come?"

"No—yes—I don't know," said Betty.

"If they're witches or gypsies we shall smash the windows. They've no right—people like that—to send children to this school."

"Ella and I will come," said Betty, and she put her

lips together. She wouldn't let anyone smash Olga's windows. Her brother Jim, the midshipman, was home on leave; she'd make him come. Who cared if Olga's people sold clothes pegs! Olga was a dear.

Up through the hayfield came the conspirators. Betty and Ella and Jim were together. There was the caravan at last, looking ghostly in the evening summer light, and there upon the steps sat Tommy Darrington. Just behind him there was the bent, dark man, and he was playing on a violin. From the tent there came a fairy dressed in something that floated and shimmered. She glided to the steps of the caravan and began to sway. The violin laughed and sobbed, and the fairy danced and danced.

"It's Olga, and she is a fairy then!" said Betty.

The violinist rose; his back was very crooked. Someone in the hayfield cried: "They're witches. Look—he's humped!" And threw a stone. The dancer ran into the caravan.

Betty, Jim, and Ella rose. "Stop that!" cried Jim, in what should have been a splendid naval voice, only it would end in a squeak, because Jim's voice was breaking.

"Mind your own business," cried the stone-thrower. "We're not going to have mad people here, coming to our school!"

Jim and the boy who had thrown grappled with each other; Tommy Darrington stood up and shut the caravan steps and the caravan door, standing against it, outside, waving his crutch.

"Come on!" he cried. "Come on, if you dare!"

No one came; they could hear Jim and the other boy scuffling, pummeling; they could hear unearthly music; and had seen fairy dancing; they were scared; they were angry because they were scared. Under the hedgerow were stones, cleared from the field; some of the children picked them up and threw them at the caravan; many missed, some pattered on the caravan; one hit Tommy.

The evening had clouded over and it was getting dark. A light suddenly appeared in the caravan. The door was opened and a woman stood on the steps. A little cry of amazement went up from the children. It was Miss Bolt, their schoolmistress.

No more stones were thrown. Jim Croft hit his opponent on the nose again and let him go. Miss Bolt just stood there, looking toward them. Nearly everyone ran away. Betty and Ella thought of going to see Miss Bolt and saying they had come to save the caravan, not attack it, but that seemed like boasting. They, too, turned around and went away.

In school next morning most of the children looked worried. If you spent the evening throwing stones at the roof that happened to shelter your schoolmistress, what happened to you? Olga Gray did not appear; Tommy Darrington did not appear.

When Miss Bolt came she said: "Children, your fairy opera performance won't take place. Up to last night I hoped that Sir Gilbert Gray, a world-famous musician, and Olga's father, would help us. By your own actions you have now made that impossible."

A gasp went round the school. Ida Burman murmured: "She should have told us."

Miss Bolt said: "Olga feared to seem superior. She wanted to make friends of you."

Betty Croft said: "Oh, Miss Bolt, isn't she coming any more?"

Miss Bolt shook her head. "No," she said. "The violinist, who is an old friend of Sir Gilbert's, thinks it better to find a more hospitable valley. They are taking Tommy with them—Sir Gilbert thinks he knows a surgeon who can cure Tommy's leg."

"Teacher, we didn't know."

Miss Bolt rapped the desk. "Know!" she said, "Couldn't you have trusted?" Her eyes rested on Tommy's empty place and softened. "It's better to believe in fairies and take things on trust," she said. "We'll miss the singing lesson. Get out your arithmetic books. Ida Burman, there were three sums wrong in your homework book; you will stay behind and get them right. Billy, close the door—I do not think we wish to see the hills today."

"No, miss," said Billy mournfully. As he closed the door, he thought he heard the creaking of a caravan upon the distant track.

# A French Lesson

From *A Little Princess*
by Frances Hodgson Burnett

When Sara entered the schoolroom the next morning everybody looked at her with interested eyes. By that time every pupil had heard a great deal about her. They knew that she was Miss Minchin's show pupil. One or two of them had even caught a glimpse of her French maid, Mariette, who had arrived the evening before. Lavinia had managed to pass Sara's room when the door was open, and had seen Mariette opening a box which had arrived late from some shop.

# ALONE IN THE WORLD

"It was full of petticoats with lace frills on them," she whispered to her friend Jessie as she bent over her geography. "I heard Miss Minchin say to Miss Amelia that her clothes were too grand for a child. My mamma says that children should be dressed simply. She has got one of those petticoats on now. I saw it when she sat down."

"She has silk stockings on!" whispered Jessie, bending over her geography also. "And what little feet! I never saw such little feet."

"Oh," sniffed Lavinia, spitefully, "that is the way her slippers are made. My mamma says that even big feet can be made to look small if you have a clever shoemaker. I don't think she is pretty at all. Her eyes are such a queer color."

"She isn't pretty as other pretty people are," said Jessie,

stealing a glance across the room; "but she makes you want to look at her again. She has very long eyelashes, but her eyes are almost green."

Sara was sitting quietly in her seat. She had been placed near Miss Minchin's desk. She was not abashed at all by the many pairs of eyes watching her. She was interested and looked back quietly at the children who looked at her. She wondered what they were thinking of, and if they liked Miss Minchin, and if they cared for their lessons, and if any of them had a papa at all like her own. She had had a long talk with Emily about her papa that morning.

"He is on the sea now, Emily," she had said. "We

47

must be very great friends to each other and tell each other things. Emily, you have the nicest eyes I ever saw. But I wish you could speak."

After Mariette had dressed her in her dark-blue schoolroom frock and tied her hair with a dark-blue ribbon, she went to Emily, who sat in a chair of her own, and gave her a book. "You can read that while I am downstairs," she said; and, seeing Mariette looking at her curiously, she spoke to her with a serious little face.

"What I believe about dolls," she said, "is that they can do things they will not let us know about. Perhaps, really, Emily can read and talk and walk, but she will only do it when people are out of the room. You see, if people knew that dolls could do things, they would make them work. So, perhaps, they have promised each other to keep it a secret. If you stay in the room, Emily will just sit there; but if you go out, she will begin to read, or go and look out of the window. Then if she heard either of us coming, she would run back, and jump into her chair and pretend she had been there all the time."

"What an odd child!" Mariette said to herself. But she had already begun to like this little girl who had an intelligent face and perfect manners. Sara had a gentle way of saying, "If you please, Mariette," which was very charming. Mariette told the head housemaid that she thanked her as if she was thanking a lady. "She has the air of a princess, this little one," she said. Indeed, she was pleased with her new little mistress and liked her place greatly.

After Sara had sat in her seat in the schoolroom for a few minutes, being looked at by the pupils, Miss Minchin rapped in a dignified manner upon her desk.

"Young ladies," she said, "I wish to introduce you to your new companion." All the girls rose in their places, and Sara rose also. "I shall expect you all to be very agreeable to Miss Crewe. As soon as lessons are over you must make each other's acquaintance."

The pupils bowed, and Sara made a curtsy, and then they sat down and looked at each other again.

"Sara," said Miss Minchin in her schoolroom manner, "come here to me." She had taken a book from the desk and was turning over its leaves. Sara went to her politely.

"As your papa has engaged a French maid for you," she began, "I conclude that he wishes you to make a special study of the French language."

Sara felt a little awkward. "I think he engaged her," she said, "because he—he thought I would like her, Miss Minchin."

"I am afraid," said Miss Minchin, with a slightly sour smile, "that you have been a very spoiled little girl and always imagine that things are done because you like them. My impression is that your papa wished you to learn French."

If Sara had been older, she could have explained herself in a very few words. But, as it was, she felt a flush rising on her cheeks. Miss Minchin was a severe and imposing person, and she seemed so sure that Sara knew nothing whatever of French that she felt as if it would be almost rude to correct her. The truth was that Sara could not remember the time when she had not seemed to know French. Her father had spoken it to her when she had been a baby. Her mother had been a French woman, and Captain Crewe had loved her language, so Sara had always heard and been familiar with it.

"I—I have never really learned French, but—but—" she began, trying shyly to make herself clear.

One of Miss Minchin's chief secret annoyances was that she did not speak French herself, and she wished to conceal the irritating fact. She, therefore had no intention of discussing the matter and laying herself open to questioning by a new pupil.

"That is enough," she said with polite tartness. "If you have not learned, you must begin at once. The French master, Monsieur Dufarge, will be here in a few minutes. Take this book and look at it until he arrives. Now, return to your desk."

Sara's cheeks felt warm. She went back to her seat and opened the book. She looked at the first page with a grave face. She knew it would be rude to smile, and she was very determined not to be rude. But it was very odd to find herself expected to study a page which told her that "*le pere*" meant "the father," and "*la mere*" meant "the mother."

"When Monsieur Dufarge comes," she thought, "I can make him understand."

Monsieur Dufarge arrived very shortly afterward. He was a very nice, intelligent, middle-aged Frenchman, and he looked interested when his eyes fell upon Sara.

"Is this a new pupil for me, madame?" he said to Miss Minchin. "I hope that is my good fortune."

"Her papa—Captain Crewe—is very anxious that she should begin the language. But I am afraid she has a childish prejudice against it. She does not seem to wish to learn," said Miss Minchin.

"I am sorry of that, mademoiselle," he said kindly to Sara. "Perhaps, when we begin to study together, I may show you that it is a charming tongue."

Little Sara rose in her seat. She was beginning to feel rather desperate, as if she were in disgrace. She looked up into Monsieur Dufarge's face with her green-gray eyes, and they were quite appealing. She knew that he would understand as soon as she spoke. She began to explain in pretty and fluent French. Madame had not understood. She had not learned French exactly—not out of books—but her papa had always spoken it to her, and she had read it and written it as she had read and written English. Her papa loved it, because her dear mamma, who had died when she was born, had been French. She would be glad to learn anything monsieur would teach her, but she had tried to explain to madame that she already knew the words in this book—and she held out the little book of phrases.

When she began to speak Miss Minchin started violently and sat staring at her over her glasses, until she had finished. Monsieur Dufarge began to smile, and his smile was one of great pleasure. To hear this pretty voice speaking his language so charmingly made him feel almost as if he were in his native land—which in foggy days in London sometimes seemed worlds away. When she had finished, he took the phrase book from her, with a look almost affectionate. But he spoke to Miss Minchin.

"Ah, madame," he said, "there is not much I can teach her. She has not learned French; she is French.

Her accent is exquisite."

"You ought to have told me," exclaimed
Miss Minchin, much mortified, turning to Sara.

"I—I tried," said Sara. "I—I suppose I did not
begin right."

Miss Minchin knew she had tried, and that it
had not been her fault that she was not allowed to
explain. And when she saw that the pupils had been
listening and that Lavinia and Jessie were giggling
behind their French grammars, she felt infuriated.

"Silence, young ladies!" she said severely, rapping
upon the desk. "Silence at once!"

And she began from that minute to feel rather a
grudge against her show pupil.

# Two Visits and What Came of Them

From *Heidi*
by Johanna Spyri

*Aged five, the orphan Heidi is taken by her cousin to live with her grandfather, a herdsman who lives up the side of a mountain in the Swiss Alps. Grandfather and Heidi live contentedly until the outside world intrudes and threatens to separate them.*

Quickly the winter passed, and still more quickly the bright glad summer, and now another winter was drawing to its close. Heidi was as light-hearted as the birds, and looked forward with more delight each day to the coming spring.

Heidi was now in her eighth year; she had learned all kinds of useful things from her grandfather; she knew how to look after the goats as well as any one, and Little Swan and Bear would follow her like two faithful dogs, giving bleats of pleasure when they heard her voice. Twice during the course of this last winter Peter had brought up a message from the schoolmaster at Dorfli, who sent word to Alm-Uncle that he ought to send Heidi to school. Uncle had sent word back each time that the schoolmaster would find him at home if he had anything he wished to say to him, but that he did not intend to send Heidi to school.

When the March sun had melted the snow on the mountain side and the snowdrops were peeping out all over the valley, and the fir trees had shaken off their burden of snow and were again waving their branches in the air, Heidi ran backward and forward with delight first to the goat-shed then to the fir-trees, and then to the hut-door, in order to let her grandfather know how much larger a piece of green there was under the trees, and then would run off to look again, for she could hardly wait till everything was green and the full summer had clothed the mountain with grass and flowers.

As Heidi was running about one sunny March morning, and had just jumped over the water-trough for the tenth time, she nearly fell backward into it with fright, for there in front of her, looking gravely at her, stood an old gentleman dressed in black. When he saw how startled she was, he said in a kind voice, "Don't be afraid of me. You must be Heidi; where is your grandfather?"

"He is sitting by the table, making wooden spoons," Heidi told him, as she opened the door.

He was the old village pastor from Dorfli who had been a neighbor of Uncle's when he lived down there. He stepped inside the hut, and going up to the old man, who was bending over his work, said,

"Good morning, neighbor."

The grandfather looked up in surprise, and then rising said, "Good morning" in return. He pushed a chair toward the visitor as he continued, "If you do not mind a wooden seat there is one for you."

The pastor sat down. "I have come today to talk over something with you," he said. "I think you know already what it is that has brought me here," and as he spoke he looked toward the child who was standing at the door, gazing with interest and surprise at the stranger.

"Heidi, go to the goats," said her grandfather. Take them some salt and stay there till I come." Heidi vanished on the spot.

"The child ought to have been at school a year ago, and most certainly this last winter," said the pastor. "The schoolmaster sent you word about it. What are you thinking of doing with the child?"

"I am thinking of not sending her to school," was the answer.

The visitor looked across at the old man, who was sitting with his arms crossed and a determined expression about his whole person. "How are you going to let her grow up then?" he asked.

"I am going to let her grow up and be happy among the goats and birds; with them she is safe, and will learn nothing evil."

"But the child is not a goat, she is a human being. She ought not to grow up in ignorance, and it is time she began her lessons. I have come now that you may have leisure to think over it, and to arrange about it during the summer. This is the last winter that she must be allowed to run wild; next winter she must come regularly to school every day."

"She will do no such thing," said the old man.

"Do you mean that by no persuasion can you be brought to see reason?" said the pastor, growing somewhat angry. "You have been about the world, and must have learned much, and I should have given you credit for more sense, neighbor."

"Indeed," replied the old man, and there was a tone in his voice that betrayed a growing irritation on his part too, "and does the worthy pastor really mean that he would wish me next winter to send a child like that some miles down the mountain through storms, and let her return at night, when even we would run a risk of being buried in the snow? And perhaps he may not have forgotten the child's mother, Adelaide? She was a sleep-walker, and had fits. Might not the child be attacked in the same way if obliged to over-exert herself? I will go before all the courts of justice in the country, and then we shall see who will force me to do it!"

"You are quite right, neighbor," said the pastor in a friendly tone of voice. "It would have been impossible to send the child to school from here. But I perceive that the child is dear to you; for her sake come down into Dorfli and live again among your fellowmen. If anything were to happen to you up here who would there be to help you? I cannot think but what you must be half frozen to death in this hut in the winter, and I do not know how the child lives through it!"

"The child has young blood in her veins and a good roof over her head, and let me further tell the pastor, that I know where wood is to be found, and when is the proper time to fetch it; the pastor can go and look inside my woodshed; the fire is never out in my hut the whole winter through. As to going to live below that is far from my thoughts; the people despise me and I them; it is therefore best for all of us that we live apart."

"No, no, it is not best for you," said the pastor in an earnest voice. "As to the people down there looking on you with dislike, it is not as bad as you think. Seek to make your peace with God, pray for forgiveness where you need it, and then come and see how differently people will look upon you, and how happy you may yet be."

The pastor had risen and stood holding out his

hand to the old man as he added with earnestness, "I will wager, neighbor, that next winter you will be down among us again, and we shall be good neighbors as of old. Give me your hand and promise me that you will come and live with us again and become reconciled to God and man."

Alm-Uncle gave the pastor his hand and answered him firmly, "You mean well, but I say now what I shall continue to say, that I will not send the child to school nor come and live among you."

"Then God help you!" said the pastor, and he left the hut and went down the mountain.

Alm-Uncle was out of humor. When Heidi said as usual that afternoon, "Can we go down to grandmother now?" he answered, "Not today." The following morning when Heidi again asked the same question, he replied, "We will see."

But before the dinner bowls had been cleared away another visitor arrived, and this time it was Cousin Dete. She had a fine feathered hat on her head, and a long skirt to her dress which swept the floor, and on the floor of a goatherd's hut there are all sorts of things that do not belong to a dress.

The grandfather looked her up and down without uttering a word. But Dete was prepared with an exceedingly amiable speech and began at once to praise the looks of the child. She was looking so well she should hardly have known her again, and it was evident that she had been well-cared for with her grandfather; but she had never lost sight of the idea of taking the child back again, for she well understood that the little one must be much in his way. Day and night she had thought over the means of placing the child somewhere, and she had just heard of something that would be a lucky chance for Heidi beyond her hopes.

Some wealthy relatives of the people she was serving had an only daughter, an invalid, who was obliged to go about in a wheeled chair. She was very much alone and had no one to share her lessons. Her father had spoken to Dete's mistress about finding a companion for her. The housekeeper had described the sort of child they wanted, simple-minded and unspoiled. Dete had thought at once of Heidi, and after Dete had given a description of Heidi, she had immediately agreed to take her. And no one could tell what good fortune there might not be in store for Heidi, for if these people took a fancy to her, why then the most unheard of luck—

"Have you nearly finished what you had to say?" broke in Alm-Uncle, who had allowed her to talk on uninterruptedly so far.

"Ugh!" exclaimed Dete, throwing up her head in disgust, "one would think I had been talking to you about the most ordinary matter; why there is not one person in all Prattigau who would not thank God if I were to bring them such a piece of news."

"You may take your news to anybody you like, I will have nothing to do with it."

But now Dete leaped up from her seat and cried, "The child is eight years old and knows nothing. You will not send her to church or school, and she is my own sister's child. I am responsible for what happens to her, and when there is such a good opening for a child, only a person who never wishes good to anyone would think of not jumping at it. But I am not going to give in, and that I tell you. I have everybody in Dorfli on my side. There is not one person there who will not take my part against you; and I advise you to think well before bringing it into court, if that is your intention; there are certain things which might be brought up against you which you would not care to hear."

"Be silent!" thundered the Uncle, and his eyes flashed with anger. "Go and be done with you!

Never let me see you again with your hat and feather, and such words on your tongue!" And with that he strode out of the hut.

"You have made grandfather angry," said Heidi, and her dark eyes had anything but a friendly expression in them as she looked at Dete.

"He will soon be all right again; come now," said Dete hurriedly. "Show me where your clothes are."

"I am not coming," said Heidi.

"Nonsense," continued Dete; then altering her tone to one half-coaxing, half-cross, "Come, come, you do not understand; you will have all sorts of good things that you never dreamed of." Then she went to the cupboard and taking out Heidi's things rolled them up in a bundle.

"I am not coming," repeated Heidi.

"Don't be so stupid and obstinate, like a goat. Listen to me: you saw your grandfather was angry and heard what he said, that he did not wish to see us ever again. He wants you now to go away with me and you must not make him angrier still. If you do not like it you can come back again."

"Can I return at once and be back home again here this evening?" asked Heidi.

"I tell you that you can come back here when you like. Today we shall go as far as Mayenfeld, and early tomorrow we shall start in the train, and that will bring you home again in no time when you wish it, for it goes as fast as the wind."

Dete had now got the bundle into her bag and the child by the hand, and so they went down the mountain together.

As it was still too early in the year to take his goats out, Peter continued to go to school at Dorfli, but now and again he stole a holiday, for he could see no use in learning to read, while to wander about a bit and look for stout sticks which might be wanted some day he thought a far better employment. As Dete and Heidi neared the grandmother's hut they met Peter coming around the corner; he had evidently been well rewarded that day for his labors, for he was carrying an immense bundle of long thick hazel sticks on his shoulders. He stood still and stared at the two approaching figures; as they came up to him, he exclaimed, "Where are you going, Heidi?"

"I am only just going over to Frankfurt for a little visit with Dete," she replied; "but I must first run in to grandmother, she will be expecting me."

"No, you must not stop," said Dete, holding Heidi, who was struggling to get away, by the hand. "You can go in when you come back," and she pulled Heidi on, fearing that Heidi might take it into her head again that she did not wish to come, and that the grandmother might stand by her.

Peter ran into the hut and banged against the table with his bundle of sticks, and his grandmother leaped up with a cry of alarm from her spinning wheel. "What is the matter?" cried the frightened old woman, while his mother, who had also started up from her seat at the shock, said "What is it, Peter? Why do you behave so roughly?"

"Because she is taking Heidi away," said Peter.

"Who? Who? Where to, Peter, where to?" asked the grandmother; but even as she spoke she guessed what had happened, for Brigitta had told her shortly before that she had seen Dete going up to Alm-Uncle. The old woman rose and opened the window and called out beseechingly, "Dete, Dete, do not take the child from us!"

The two who were hastening down the mountain heard her voice, and Dete evidently caught the words, for she grasped Heidi's hand more firmly. Heidi struggled to get free, crying, "Grandmother is calling, I must go to her."

But Dete had no intention of letting the child go, and quieted her as best she could; they must make haste now, she said, or they would be too late and not able to go on the next day to Frankfurt. But if Heidi wanted to return home she could do so at once, and then she could take something she liked back to grandmother. This was a new idea to Heidi, and it pleased her so much that Dete had no longer any difficulty in getting her along.

After a few minutes' silence, Heidi asked, "What could I take back to her?"

"We must think of something nice," answered Dete; "a soft roll of white bread, for now she is old she can hardly eat the hard, black bread."

"No, she gives it to Peter, telling him it is too hard," affirmed Heidi. "Do let us make haste, for then perhaps we can get back soon from Frankfurt, and I shall be able to give her the bread today." And Heidi started off running so that Dete with the bag under her arm could scarcely keep up.

But she was glad to get along so quickly, for they were nearing Dorfli, where her friends would probably question in a way that might put other ideas into Heidi's head. So she went on through the village, holding Heidi tightly by the hand. To all their questions she made answer, "I can't stop now, I must make haste as we have some way to go."

"Are you taking her away?" "Is she running away from Alm-Uncle?" "It's a wonder she is still alive!" Such were the words which rang out on all sides, and Dete was thankful that she had not to stop and give any distinct answers to them, while Heidi hurried eagerly forward without saying a word.

From that day forward Alm-Uncle looked more forbidding than ever when he came down and passed through Dorfli. He spoke to no one, and looked such an ogre as he came along with his pack of cheeses on his back, his stick in his hand, and his thick, frowning eyebrows, that the women would call to their little ones, "Take care! Get out of

Alm-Uncle's way or he may hurt you!"

The old man took no notice of anybody as he strode through the village on his way to the valley below, where he sold his cheeses and bought what bread and meat he wanted for himself. After he had passed the villagers each had something to say about him; how much wilder he looked than usual, how now he would not even respond to anybody's greeting, while they all agreed that it was a great mercy the child had got away from him, and had they not all noticed how the child had hurried along as if afraid that her grandfather might be following to take her back?

Only the blind grandmother would have nothing to say against him, and told those who came to her to bring her work, or take away what she had spun, how kind he had been with the child, how good to her and her daughter, and how many afternoons he had spent mending the house which, but for his help, would certainly by this time have fallen down over their heads. All this was repeated down in Dorfli; but most people who heard it said that grandmother was too old to understand, and very likely had not heard rightly what was said; as she was blind she was probably also deaf.

Alm-Uncle went no more now to the grandmother's house, and it was well that he had made it so safe, for it was not touched again for a long time. The days were sad again now for the old blind woman, and not one passed but what she would murmur complainingly, "Alas! all our happiness and pleasure have gone with the child, and now the days are so long and dreary! Pray God, I see Heidi again once more before I die!"

# NEW FRIENDS

# Ginger

From *Black Beauty*
by Anna Sewell

*Black Beauty is written as the autobiography of a young horse.
At the beginning of this extract he has just met Ginger, a chestnut
filly who was to become a lifelong companion, and all is well
in his life as he has a good and kind owner.*

One day when Ginger and I were standing alone
in the shade, she wanted to know all about my
bringing up and breaking in, and I told her.

"Well," said she, "if I had had your bringing up I
might have had as good a temper as you, but now
I don't believe I ever shall."

"Why not?" I said.

"Because it has been all so different with me," she replied. "I never had any one, horse or man, that was kind to me, or that I cared to please. I was taken from my mother as soon as I was weaned, and put with lots of other young colts; none of them cared for me, and I cared for none of them. There was no kind master to look after me, and bring me nice things to eat. The man that had the care of us never gave me a kind word. I do not mean that he ill-used me, but he did not care for us one bit further than to see that we had plenty to eat, and shelter.

"A footpath ran through our field, and very often the boys passing through would fling stones to make us gallop. One fine young colt was badly cut in the face. We settled it in our minds that boys were our enemies.

"But when it came to breaking in, that was a bad time for me; several men came to catch me, and when at last they closed me in at one corner of the field, one caught me by the forelock, another caught me by the nose and held it so tight I could hardly draw my breath; then another took my under jaw in his hard hand and wrenched my mouth open, and so by force they got on the halter and the bar into my mouth; then one dragged me along by the halter, another flogging behind, and this was the first experience I had of men's kindness; it was all force. They did not give me a chance to know what they wanted. I had a great deal of spirit, and was very wild, and gave them, I dare say, plenty of trouble, but then it was dreadful to be shut up in a stall day after day instead of having my liberty, and I fretted and pined and wanted to get loose.

"There was one—the old master, Mr Ryder— who, I think, could soon have brought me round, and could have done anything with me; but he had given up all the hard part of the trade to his son and to another experienced man, and he only came at times to oversee.

"His son was a strong, tall, bold man; they called him Samson, and he used to boast that he had never found a horse that could throw him. There was no gentleness in him, but only hardness, a hard voice, a hard eye, a hard hand; and I felt from the first that what he wanted was to wear all the spirit out of me, and just make me into a quiet, humble, obedient piece of horseflesh. "Horseflesh!" Yes, that is all that he thought about," and Ginger stamped her foot as if the thought of him made her angry.

Then she went on: "If I did not do exactly what he wanted he would get put out, and make me run around with that long rein in the training field till he had tired me out.

"One day he had worked me hard in every way he could, and when I lay down I was tired, and miserable, and angry; it all seemed so hard. The next morning he came for me early, and ran me around again for a long time. I had scarcely had an hour's rest, when he came again for me with a saddle and bridle and a new kind of bit. I could never quite tell how it came about; he had only just mounted me on the training ground, when something I did put him out of temper, and he chucked me hard with the rein. The new bit was very painful, and I reared up suddenly, which angered him still more, and he began to flog me.

"I felt my whole spirit set against him. I began to kick, and plunge, and rear as I had never done before; for a long time he stuck to the saddle and punished me cruelly with his whip and spurs, but I cared for nothing he could do if only I could get him off. At last after a terrible struggle I threw him off backward. I heard him fall heavily on the turf, and without looking behind me, I galloped off to the other end of the field; there I turned around and saw my persecutor slowly rising from the ground and going into the stable.

"I stood under an oak tree and watched, but no one came to catch me. The time went on, and the

sun was very hot; the flies swarmed around me and settled on my bleeding flanks where the spurs had dug in. I felt hungry, for I had not eaten since the early morning, but there was not enough grass in that meadow for a goose to live on.

"I wanted to lie down and rest, but with the saddle strapped on there was no comfort. The afternoon wore on. I saw the other colts led in, and I knew they were having a good feed.

"At last, just as the sun went down, I saw the old master come out with a sieve in his hand. He was a very fine old gentleman with quite white hair, but his voice was what I should know him by among a thousand. It was not high, nor yet low, but full, and clear, and kind, and when he gave orders it was so steady and decided that every one knew, both horses and men, that he expected to be obeyed.

"He came quietly along, shaking the oats that he had in the sieve, and speaking cheerfully and gently to me: "Come along, lassie; come along." I stood still and let him come up; he held the oats to me, and I began to eat without fear. He stood by, patting and stroking me while I was eating, and seeing the clots of blood on my side he seemed very vexed. "Poor lassie! it was a bad business;" then he quietly took the rein and led me to the stable. At the door stood Samson. I laid my ears back and snapped at him. "Stand back," said the master, "and keep out of her way; you've done a bad day's work for this filly." He growled something about a vicious brute. "Hark ye," said the father, "a bad-tempered man will never make a good-tempered horse. You've not learned your trade yet, Samson."

"Then he led me into my box, took off the saddle and bridle with his own hands, and tied me up; then he called for a pail of warm water and a sponge, took off his coat, and while the stable-man held the pail, he sponged my sides so tenderly that I was sure he knew how sore and bruised they were. "Whoa! my pretty one," he said, "stand still, stand still." His very voice did me good, and the bathing was very comfortable. The skin was so broken at the corners of my mouth that I could not eat the hay. He looked closely at it, shook his head, and told the man to fetch a good bran mash and put some meal into it. How good that mash was! So soft and healing to my mouth. He stood by all the time I was eating, stroking me, and talking to the man. "If a high-mettled creature like this," said he, "can't be broken by fair means, she will never be good for anything."

"After that he often came to see me, and when my mouth was healed the other breaker, Job, went on training me; he was steady and thoughtful, and I soon learned what he wanted." And so Ginger finished telling me about her bad start in life.

# The Key
# to the Garden

From *The Secret Garden*
by Frances Hodgson Burnett

*Mary Lennox is the spoiled orphan daughter of a British official in
India who is brought back to Misselthwaite Manor in Yorkshire,
England, to live with her uncle, a disabled and reclusive man.*

When Mary opened her eyes she sat upright in
bed immediately, and called to Martha.

"Look at the moor! Look at the moor!"

The rainstorm had ended and the gray mist and
clouds had been swept away in the night by the
wind. The wind had ceased and a brilliant, deep
blue sky arched high over the moorland. Never had

Mary dreamed of a sky so blue. In India skies were hot and blazing; this was a deep cool blue which almost seemed to sparkle like the waters of some lovely bottomless lake. Here and there, high in the arched blueness floated small clouds of snow-white fleece. The far-reaching world of the moor itself looked softly blue instead of gloomy purple-black or dreary gray.

"Aye," said Martha with a cheerful grin. "Th' storm's over for a bit. It does like this at this time o' th' year. It goes off in a night like it was pretendin' it had never been here an' never meant to come again. That's because th' springtime's on its way. It's a long way off yet, but it's comin'."

"I thought perhaps it always rained or looked dark in England," Mary said.

"Eh! no!" said Martha, sitting up on her heels among her black lead brushes. "Nowt o' th' soart!"

"What does that mean?" asked Mary seriously. In India, natives spoke different dialects which only a few people understood, so she was not surprised when Martha used words she did not know.

"There now," Martha said. "I've talked broad Yorkshire again like Mrs. Medlock said I mustn't. "Nowt o' th' soart" means "nothin'-of-the-sort,"" slowly and carefully, "but it takes so long to say it. Yorkshire's th' sunniest place on earth when it is sunny. I told thee tha'd like th' moor after a bit. Just you wait till you see th' gold-colored gorse blossoms an' th' blossoms o' th' broom, an' th' heather flowerin', all purple bells, an' hundreds o' butterflies flutterin' an' bees hummin' an' skylarks soarin' up an' singin'. You'll want to get out on it as sunrise an' live out on it all day like Dickon does."

"Could I ever get there?" asked Mary wistfully, looking through her window at the far-off blue.

"I don't know," said Martha. "Tha's never used tha' legs since tha' was born, it seems. Tha' couldn't walk five mile. It's five mile to our cottage."

"I should like to see your cottage."

Martha stared at her a moment curiously before she took up her polishing brush again. She was thinking that the small plain face did not look quite as sour as it had done the first morning she saw it.

"I'll ask my mother about it," she said. "She's one o' them that nearly always sees a way to do things. It's my day out today an' I'm goin' home. Eh! I am glad. Mrs Medlock thinks a lot o' mother. Perhaps she could talk to her."

"I like your mother," said Mary.

"I should think tha' did," agreed Martha, polishing away.

"I've never seen her," said Mary.

"No, tha' hasn't," replied Martha.

She sat up on her heels again and rubbed the end of her nose with the back of her hand as if puzzled for a moment, but she ended quite positively.

"Well, she's that sensible an' hard workin' an' goodnatured an' clean that no one could help likin' her whether they'd seen her or not. When I'm goin' home to her on my day out I just jump for joy when I'm crossin' the moor."

"I like Dickon," added Mary, "And I've never seen him."

"Well," said Martha stoutly, "I've told thee that th' birds likes him an' th' rabbits an' wild sheep an' ponies, an' th' foxes. I wonder," staring at her reflectively, "what Dickon would think of thee?"

"He wouldn't like me," said Mary in her stiff, cold little way. "No one does."

Martha looked reflective again.

"How does tha' like thysel'?" she inquired, really quite as if she were curious to know.

Mary hesitated and thought it over. "Not at all, really," she answered. "But I never thought of that before."

Martha grinned a little as if at some homely recollection. "Mother said that to me once," she said. "She was at her wash-tub an' I was in a bad temper an' talkin' ill of folk, an' she says: "Tha' young vixen, tha'! There tha' stands sayin' tha' doesn't like this one an' tha' doesn't like that one. How does tha' like thysel'?" It made me laugh an' it brought me to my senses in a minute."

# The Key to the Garden

She went away in high spirits as soon as she had given Mary her breakfast. She was going to walk five miles across the moor to the cottage, and she was going to help her mother with the washing and do the week's baking and enjoy herself thoroughly.

Mary went out into the garden as quickly as possible, and the first thing she did was to run around the fountain flower garden ten times. When she had finished she felt better. She went into the first kitchen-garden and found Ben Weatherstaff there with two other gardeners. The change in the weather seemed to have done him good. He spoke to her of his own accord. "Spring's comin'," he said.

"Cannot tha' smell it?"

Mary sniffed and thought she could. "I smell something nice and fresh and damp," she said.

"That's th' good rich earth," he answered, digging away. "It's glad when plantin' time comes. It's dull in th' winter when it's got nowt to do. In th' flower gardens out there you'll see bits o' green spikes stickin' out o' th' earth after a bit."

"What will they be?" asked Mary.

"Crocuses, snowdrops, an' daffydowndillys. Has tha' never seen them?"

"No. Everything is hot, and wet, and green after the rains in India," said Mary. "And I think things grow up in a night."

"These won't grow up in a night," said Weatherstaff. "Tha'll have to wait for 'em. They'll poke up a bit higher here, an' push out a spike more there, an' uncurl a leaf this day an' another that. You watch 'em."

"I am going to," answered Mary.

# The Key to the Garden

Very soon she heard the soft rustling flight of wings again and she knew at once that the robin had come again. He was very pert and lively, and hopped briskly about so close to her feet that she asked Ben Weatherstaff, "Do you think he remembers me?"

"Remembers thee!" said Ben Weatherstaff indignantly. "He knows every cabbage stump in th' gardens, let alone th' people. He's never seen a little girl here before, an' he's bent on findin' out all about thee."

"Are things stirring down below in the dark in that garden where he lives?" Mary inquired.

"What garden?" grunted Ben Weatherstaff, becoming surly again.

"The one where the old rose-trees are." She could not help asking, she wanted so much to know. "Are all the flowers dead, or do some of them come again in the summer? Are there any roses?"

"Ask him," said Ben Weatherstaff, hunching his

shoulders toward the robin. "He's the only one as knows. No one else has seen inside it for ten year'."

Ten years was a long time, Mary thought. She had been born ten years ago.

She walked away, slowly thinking. She had begun to like the garden just as she had begun to like the robin and Dickon and Martha's mother. She was beginning to like Martha, too. That seemed a good many people to like—when you were not used to liking. She thought of the robin as one of the people. She went to her walk outside the long, ivy-covered wall over which she could see the treetops; and the second time she walked up and down the most interesting and exciting thing happened to her.

She heard a chirp and a twitter, and when she looked at the bare flowerbed at her left side there he was hopping about and pretending to peck things out of the earth to persuade her that he had not followed her. But she knew he had followed her and the surprise so filled her with delight that she almost trembled a little.

"You do remember me!" she cried out. "You do! You are prettier than anything else in the world!"

She talked and coaxed, and he hopped and flirted his tail and twittered. It was as if he were talking. He allowed her to draw closer and closer to him, and bend down and talk and try to make something like robin sounds.

To think that he should actually let her come as near to him as that! He knew nothing in the world would make her put out her hand toward him or startle him in the tiniest way. He knew it because he was a real person—only nicer than any other person in the world. The flower-bed was not quite bare. It was bare of flowers, but there were tall shrubs and low ones which grew together at the back of the bed, and as the robin hopped about under them she saw him hop over a small pile of freshly turned up earth. He stopped on it to look for a worm. The earth had been turned up because a dog had been trying to dig up a mole and he had scratched quite a deep hole.

Mary looked at it, not really knowing why the hole was there, and as she looked she saw something almost buried in the newly-turned soil. It was something like a ring of rusty iron or brass and when the robin flew up into a tree nearby she put out her hand and picked the ring up. It was more than a ring, however; it was an old key that looked as if it had been buried a long time.

Mistress Mary stood up and looked at it with an almost frightened face as it hung from her finger. "Perhaps it has been buried for ten years," she said in a whisper. "Perhaps it is the key to the garden!"

# The Riverbank

From *The Wind in the Willows*
by Kenneth Grahame

The Mole had been working very hard all the morning, spring-cleaning his little home. First with brooms, then with dusters; then on ladders and steps and chairs, with a brush and a pail of whitewash; till he had dust in his throat and eyes, and splashes of whitewash all over his black fur, and an aching back and weary arms. Spring was moving in the air above and in the earth below and around him, penetrating even his dark and lowly little house with its spirit of divine discontent and longing.

It was small wonder, then, that he suddenly flung down his brush on the floor, said "Bother!" and "Oh blow!" and also "Hang spring-cleaning!" and bolted out of the house without even waiting to put on his coat. Something up above was calling him imperiously, and he made for the steep little tunnel, which answered in his case to the graveled carriage-drive owned by animals whose residences are nearer to the sun and air. So he worked busily with his little paws and muttering to himself, "Up we go! Up we go!" till at last, *pop!* His snout came out into the sunlight, and he found himself rolling in the warm grass of a great meadow.

"This is fine!" he said to himself. "This is better than whitewashing!" The sunshine struck hot on his fur, soft breezes caressed his heated brow, and the carol of happy birds fell on his dulled hearing almost like a shout. Jumping off all his legs at once, in the joy of living and the delight of spring without its cleaning, he pursued his way across the meadow till he reached the hedge on the further side.

Hither and thither through the meadows he rambled busily, along the hedgerows, across the copses, finding everywhere birds building, flowers budding, leaves thrusting—everything happy. And instead of having an uneasy conscience whispering "whitewash!" he somehow could only feel how jolly it was to be the only idle dog among all these busy citizens. After all, the best part of a holiday is perhaps not so much to be resting yourself, as to see all the other fellows busy working.

He thought his happiness was complete when, as he meandered aimlessly along, suddenly he stood by the edge of a full-fed river. Never in his life had he seen a river before—this sleek, sinuous, full-bodied animal, chasing and chuckling, gripping things with a gurgle, and leaving them with a laugh. All was a-shake and a-shiver—glints and gleams and sparkles, rustle and swirl, chatter and bubble. The Mole was bewitched, entranced, fascinated. By the side of the river he trotted, and when tired at last, he sat on the bank, while the river still chattered on to him, a babbling procession of the best stories in the world, sent from the heart of the earth to be told at last to the insatiable sea.

As he sat on the grass and looked across the river, a dark hole in the bank opposite, just above the water's edge, caught his eye, and dreamily he fell to considering what a nice snug dwelling-place it would make for an animal with few wants and fond of a riverside residence, above flood level and remote from noise and dust. As he gazed, something bright and small seemed to twinkle down in the heart of it, vanished, then twinkled once more like a tiny star. Then, as he looked, it winked at him, and so declared itself to be an eye, and a small face began gradually to grow up around it, like a frame around a picture.

A brown little face, with whiskers.

A grave round face, with the twinkle in its eye

# The Riverbank

that had first caught his notice.

Neat ears and thick silky hair.

It was the Water Rat!

Then the two animals stood and regarded each other cautiously.

"Hullo, Mole!" said the Water Rat.

"Hullo, Rat!" said the Mole.

"Would you like to come over?" enquired the Rat presently.

"Oh, its all very well to talk," said the Mole, rather pettishly, he being new to riverside life and its ways.

The Rat said nothing, but stooped and unfastened a rope and hauled on it; then lightly stepped into a little boat, which the Mole had not observed. It was just the size for two animals; and the Mole's whole heart went out to it at once.

The Rat sculled smartly across and made fast.
Then he held up his forepaw as the Mole stepped
gingerly down. "Lean on that!" he said. "Now then,
step lively!" and the Mole to his surprise found
himself seated in the stern of a real boat.

"This has been a wonderful day!" said he, as the
Rat shoved off and took to the sculls again. "I've
never been in a boat before in all my life."

"What?" cried the Rat, open-mouthed: "Never
been in a—you never—well I—what have you been
doing, then?"

"Is it so nice as all that?" asked the Mole shyly.

"Nice? It's the only thing," said the Water Rat
solemnly. "Believe me there is nothing half so much
worth doing as simply messing about in boats.
Simply messing..." he went on dreamily, "messing...
about... in... boats... messing..."

"Look ahead, Rat!" cried the Mole suddenly.

It was too late. The boat struck the bank full tilt.
The joyous oarsman lay on his back at the bottom

of the boat, his heels in the air.

"—about in boats or with boats," the Rat went on composedly, picking himself up with a pleasant laugh. "In or out of 'em, it doesn't matter. Whether you get away, or whether you don't; whether you arrive at your destination or whether you reach somewhere else, or whether you never get anywhere at all, you're always busy, and you never do anything in particular; and when you've done it there's always something else to do.

"Look here! If you've really nothing else on hand this morning, supposing we drop down the river together, and have a day of it?"

The Mole waggled his toes from sheer happiness, spread his chest with a sigh of full contentment, and leant back into the soft cushions. "What a day I'm having!" he said. "Let us start at once!"

"Hold hard a minute, then!" said the Rat. He looped the painter through a ring in his landing-stage, climbed up into his hole above, and after a short interval reappeared staggering under a fat, wicker luncheon-basket.

"Shove that under your feet," he observed to the Mole, as he passed it down into the boat. Then he untied the painter and took the sculls again.

"What's inside it?" asked the Mole, wriggling with curiosity.

"There's cold chicken inside it," replied the Rat briefly; "coldtonguecoldhamcoldbeefpickled gherkinssaladfrenchrollscresssandwichespottedmeat gingerbeerlemonadesodawater—"

"Oh stop, stop," cried the Mole in ecstacies: "This is too much!"

"Do you really think so?" inquired the Rat seriously. "It's only what I always take on these little excursions."

The Mole never heard a word he was saying. Absorbed in the new life he was entering upon, intoxicated with the sparkle, the ripple, the scents, and the sounds and the sunlight, he trailed a paw in the water and dreamed long waking dreams. The Water Rat, like the good little fellow he was, sculled steadily on and forebore to disturb him.

"I like your clothes awfully, old chap," he remarked after some half an hour or so had passed. "I'm going to get a black velvet smoking-suit myself some day, as soon as I can afford it."

"I beg your pardon," said the Mole, pulling himself together with an effort. "You must think me very rude, but all this is so new to me. So... this... is... a... river!"

"The River," corrected the Rat.

"And you live by the river? What a jolly life!"

"By it and with it and on it and in it," said the Rat. "It's brother and sister to me, and aunts, and company, and food and drink, and (naturally) washing. It's my world, and I don't want any other."

"But isn't it a bit dull at times?" the Mole ventured to ask. "Just you and the river, and no one else to pass a word with?"

"No one else to—well, I mustn't be hard on you," said the Rat with forbearance. "You're new to it, and of course you don't know. The bank is so crowded nowadays that many people are moving away altogether. Otters, kingfishers, dabchicks, moorhens, all of them about all day long and always wanting you to do something, as if a fellow had no business of his own to attend to!"

"What lies over there?" asked the Mole, waving a paw towards a background of woodland that darkly framed the water-meadows on one side of the river.

"Oh, that's just the Wild Wood," said the Rat shortly. "We don't go there much, we river-bankers."

"Aren't they—aren't they very nice people in there?" said the Mole, a trifle nervously.

"W-e-ll," replied the Rat, "let me see. The squirrels are all right. And the rabbits. And then there's Badger, of course. He lives right in the heart of it—wouldn't live anywhere else, either, if you paid him to do it. Dear old Badger! Nobody interferes with him. They'd better not," he added.

"Why, who should interfere with him?" asked the Mole.

"Well, of course, there are others," explained the Rat in a hesitating sort of way. "Weasels and stoats and foxes and so on. They're all right in a way—I'm very good friends with them—pass the time of day when we meet, and all that—but they break out sometimes, there's no denying it, and then—well, you can't really trust them, and that's the fact."

"And beyond the Wild Wood?" the Mole asked.

"Beyond the Wild Wood comes the Wide World," said the Rat. "And that's something that doesn't matter, either to you or me. I've never been there, and I'm never going, nor you either, if you've got any sense at all. Now then! Here's our backwater at last, where we're going to lunch."

Leaving the main stream, they now passed into what seemed at first sight like a little land-locked lake. Green turf sloped down to either edge, snaky tree-roots gleamed below the surface of the water, while ahead of them the foamy tumble of a weir, arm-in-arm with a restless dripping mill-wheel, that held up in its turn a gray-gabled mill-house, filled the air with a soothing murmur of sound. It was so very beautiful that the Mole could only hold up both forepaws and gasp, "Oh my! Oh my! Oh my!"

The Rat brought the boat alongside the bank, made her fast, helped the still awkward Mole safely ashore, and swung out the luncheon-basket. The Mole begged to be allowed to unpack it, and the Rat was very pleased to sprawl at full length on the grass and rest, while his excited friend shook out the table cloth, took out all the packets one by one and arranged their contents, still gasping, "Oh my! Oh my!" at each fresh revelation.

When all was ready, the Rat said, "Now, pitch in, old fellow!" and the Mole was indeed very glad to obey, for he had started his spring-cleaning at a very early hour that morning, as people will do, and

had not paused for bite or sup.

"What are you looking at?" said the Rat presently, when the edge of their hunger was somewhat dulled, and the Mole's eyes were able to wander off the table cloth a little.

"I am looking," said the Mole, "at a streak of bubbles that I see travelling along the surface of the water. That is a thing that strikes me as funny."

"Bubbles? Oho!" said the Rat, and chirruped cheerily in an inviting sort of way.

A broad glistening muzzle showed itself above the edge of the bank, and the Otter hauled himself out and shook the water from his coat.

"Greedy beggars!" he observed, making for the provender. "Why didn't you invite me, Ratty?"

"This was an impromptu affair," explained the Rat. "By the way—my friend Mr Mole."

"Proud, I'm sure," said the Otter, and the two animals were friends forthwith.

"Such a rumpus everywhere!" continued the

# The Riverbank

Otter. "All the world seems out on the river today. I came up this backwater to try and get a moment's peace, and stumble upon you fellows! At least—I beg pardon—I don't exactly mean that, you know."

There was a rustle behind them, proceeding from a hedge wherein last year's leaves still clung thick, and a stripy head, with high shoulders behind it, peered forth on them.

"Come on, old Badger!" shouted the Rat.

The Badger trotted forward a pace or two; then grunted, "H'm! Company," and turned his back and disappeared from view.

"That's just the sort of fellow he is!" observed the disappointed Rat. "Now we shan't see any more of him today. Well, tell us, who's out on the river?"

"Toad's out, for one," replied the Otter. "In his new wager-boat—new togs, new everything!" The two animals looked at each other and laughed.

"Once, it was nothing but sailing," said the Rat, "Then he tired of that and took to punting.

Nothing would please him but to punt all day and every day, and a nice mess he made of it. Last year it was house-boating, and we all had to go and stay with him in his house-boat, and pretend we liked it. He was going to spend the rest of his life in a house-boat. It's all the same, whatever he takes up; he gets tired of it, and starts on something fresh."

"Such a good fellow, too," remarked the Otter reflectively. "But no stability—especially in a boat!"

From where they sat they could get a glimpse of the main stream across the island that separated them; and just then a wager-boat flashed into view, the rower—a short, stout figure—splashing badly and rolling a good deal, but working his hardest.

"He'll be out of the boat in a minute if he rolls like that," said the Rat.

"Of course he will," chuckled the Otter. "Did I ever tell you that good story about Toad and the lock-keeper? It happened this way. Toad…"

An errant May-fly swerved unsteadily athwart

the current in the intoxicated fashion affected by young bloods of May-flies seeing life. A swirl of water and a *"cloop!"* and the May-fly was visible no more.

Neither was the Otter.

The Mole looked down. The voice was still in his ears, but the turf whereon he had sprawled was vacant. Not an Otter to be seen. But again there was a streak of bubbles on the surface of the river.

"Well, well," said the Rat, "I suppose we ought to be moving. I wonder which of us had better pack the luncheon-basket?" He did not speak as if he was frightfully eager for the treat.

"Oh, please let me," said the Mole. So, of course, the Rat let him.

Packing the basket was not quite such pleasant work as unpacking the basket. But the Mole was bent on enjoying everything, and although just when he had got the basket packed and strapped up tightly he saw a plate staring up at him from the grass, and when the job had been done again the Rat pointed out a fork which anybody ought to have seen, and last of all, the mustard pot, which he had been sitting on without knowing it—till, somehow, the thing got finished at last.

The afternoon sun was getting low as the Rat sculled gently homeward in a dreamy mood. But the Mole was getting restless, and presently he said, "Ratty! Please, I want to row, now!"

The Rat shook his head with a smile. "Not yet, my young friend," he said. "Wait till you've had a few lessons. It's not so easy as it looks."

The Mole was quiet for a minute or two. But he began to feel more and more jealous of Rat, sculling so strongly and so easily along, and his pride began to whisper that he could do it every bit as well. Suddenly he jumped up and seized the sculls, so abruptly, that the Rat, who was gazing dreamily out over the water, was taken by surprise and fell backward off his seat with his legs in the air, while the Mole took his place and grabbed the sculls with confidence.

"Stop it!" cried the Rat, from the bottom of the boat. "You'll have us over!"

The Mole flung his sculls back with a flourish, and made a great dig at the water. He missed the surface altogether, his legs flew up above his head, and he found himself lying on the top of the prostrate Rat. Alarmed, he made a grab at the side of the boat, and the next moment—*Sploosh!*

Over went the boat, and he found himself struggling in the river.

Oh my, how cold the water was, and how very wet it felt. How it sang in his ears as he went down, down, down! How bright and welcome the sun looked as he rose to the surface coughing and spluttering! How black was his despair when he felt himself sinking again!

Then a firm paw gripped him by the back of his neck. It was the Rat, and he was evidently laughing—the Mole could feel him laughing, right down his arm and through his paw.

The Rat got hold of a scull and shoved it under the Mole's arm; then he did the same by the other side of him and, swimming behind, propelled the helpless animal to shore, hauled him out, and set him on the bank, a squashy, pulpy lump of misery.

When the Rat had rubbed him down a bit, and wrung some of the wet out of him, he said, "Now, then, old fellow! Trot up and down the towing-path as hard as you can, till you're warm and dry again, while I dive for the luncheon-basket."

So the dismal Mole, wet without and ashamed within, trotted about till he was fairly dry, while the Rat plunged into the water again, recovered the boat, righted her, fetched his floating property to shore by degrees, and finally dived successfully for the luncheon-basket and struggled to land with it.

When all was ready for a start once more, the Mole, limp and dejected, took his seat in the stern of the boat; and as they set off, he said in a low voice, "Ratty, my generous friend! I am very sorry for my foolish and ungrateful conduct. My heart fails me when I think how I might have lost that beautiful basket. Indeed, I have been very silly, and I know it. Will you overlook it this once and forgive me, and let things go on as before?"

"That's all right, bless you!" responded the Rat cheerily. "What's a little wet to a water rat? I'm more in the water than out of it most days. Don't you think any more about it. Look here! I really think you had better come and stop with me for a little time. It's very plain and rough, you know—not like Toad's house at all—but you haven't seen that yet. Still, I can make you comfortable. And I'll teach you to row, and to swim, and you'll soon be as handy on the water as any of us."

The Mole was so touched by his kind manner that he could find no voice to answer him, and he had to brush away a tear with the back of his paw. But the Rat kindly looked in another direction, and presently the Mole's spirits revived again.

When they got home, the Rat made a bright fire in the parlor, planted the Mole in an armchair in front of it (having fetched down a dressing-gown and slippers for him), and told him river stories till supper-time. Very thrilling stories they were, too, to an earth-dwelling animal like Mole. Stories about weirs, and sudden floods, and leaping pike; about herons, and how particular they were whom they spoke to; and about adventures down drains, and night-fishings with Otter, or excursions far afield with Badger. Supper was a cheerful meal; but shortly afterward a terribly sleepy Mole had to be escorted upstairs by his considerate host, to the best bedroom, where he soon laid his head on his pillow in great peace and contentment, knowing that his new-found friend the River was lapping the sill of his window.

This day was only the first of many for the emancipated Mole, each of them longer and full of interest as the ripening summer moved onward. He learned to swim and to row, and entered into the joy of running water; and with his ear to the reed-stems he caught, at intervals, something of what the wind went whispering so constantly among them.

# The Journey Begins

From *The Wonderful Wizard of Oz*
by L. Frank Baum

*Dorothy is carried in her house by a cyclone from Kansas to the land of Oz. When her house kills the Wicked Witch, Dorothy is hailed as a friend by the Munchkins. She is told that to find her way home she must ask for the help of the Wizard of Oz, who lives in the City of Emeralds at the end of the yellow brick road.*

When Dorothy was left alone she began to feel hungry. So she went to the cupboard and cut herself some bread, which she spread with butter. She gave some to Toto, and taking a pail from the shelf she carried it down to the little brook and filled it with clear, sparkling water. Toto ran over to the trees and began to bark at the birds sitting there. Dorothy went to get him, and saw such delicious fruit hanging from the branches that she gathered some of it, finding it just what she wanted to help out her breakfast. Then she went back to the house, helped herself and Toto to a good drink of the cool water, and set about making ready for the journey to the City of Emeralds.

Dorothy had only one other dress, but that happened to be clean and was hanging on a peg beside her bed. It was gingham, with checks of white and blue. The girl washed herself, dressed in the clean gingham, and tied her pink sunbonnet on her head. She took a little basket and filled it with bread from the cupboard, laying a white cloth over the top. Then she looked down at her feet and noticed how worn her shoes were.

"They surely will never do for a long journey, Toto," she said. And Toto looked up into her face with his little black eyes and wagged his tail to show he knew what she meant.

At that moment Dorothy saw lying on the table the silver shoes that had belonged to the Witch of the East. "I wonder if they will fit me," she said to Toto. "They would be just the thing to take a long walk in, for they could not wear out."

She took off her old leather shoes and tried on the silver ones, which fitted her as well as if they had been made for her.

Finally she picked up her basket. "Come along, Toto," she said. "We will go to the Emerald City and ask the Great Oz how to get back to Kansas."

She closed the door, locked it, and put the key carefully in the pocket of her dress. And so, with Toto trotting along soberly behind her, she started on her journey.

There were several roads nearby, but it did not take her long to find the one paved with yellow bricks. Within a short time she was walking briskly toward the Emerald City, her silver shoes tinkling merrily on the hard, yellow road. The sun shone bright and the birds sang sweetly, and Dorothy did not feel nearly so bad as you might think a little girl would who had been suddenly whisked away from her own country and set down a strange land.

She was surprised, as she walked along, to see how pretty the country was about her. There were neat fences at the sides of the road, painted a dainty blue, and beyond them were fields of grain and vegetables in abundance. Evidently the Munchkins were good farmers, able to raise large crops. Once in a while she would pass a house, and the people came out to look at her and bow low as she went by; for everyone knew she had been the means of destroying the Wicked Witch and setting them free from bondage. The Munchkin houses were odd-looking dwellings, for each was round, with a big dome for a roof. All were painted blue, for in this country of the East, blue was the favorite color.

When she had gone several miles she thought she would stop to rest, and so climbed to the top of the fence beside the road and sat down. There was a great cornfield beyond the fence, and not far away she saw a Scarecrow, placed high on a pole to keep the birds from the ripe corn.

Dorothy leaned her chin upon her hand and gazed at the Scarecrow. Its head was a small sack stuffed with straw, with eyes, nose, and mouth painted on it to represent a face. An old, pointed blue hat, that had belonged to some Munchkin, was perched on his head, and the rest of the figure was a blue suit of clothes, worn and faded, which had also been stuffed with straw. On the feet were some old boots with blue tops, such as every man wore in this country, and the figure was raised above the stalks of corn by means of the pole stuck up its back.

While Dorothy was looking into the queer, painted face of the Scarecrow, she was surprised to see one of the eyes wink at her. She thought she must have been mistaken at first, for none of the scarecrows in Kansas ever wink; but presently the figure nodded its head to her in a friendly way. Then she climbed down from the fence and walked up to it, while Toto ran around the pole and barked.

"Good day," said the Scarecrow, in a husky voice.

"Did you speak?" asked the girl, in wonder.

"Certainly," answered the Scarecrow. "How do you do?"

"I'm pretty well, thank you," replied Dorothy politely. "How do you do?"

"I'm not feeling well," said the Scarecrow, with a smile, "for it is very tedious being perched up here night and day to scare away crows."

"Can't you get down?" asked Dorothy.

"No, for this pole is stuck up my back. If you will please take away the pole I shall be greatly obliged."

Dorothy reached up both arms and lifted the figure off the pole for, being stuffed with straw, it was quite light.

"Thank you very much," said the Scarecrow, when he had been set down on the ground. "I feel like a new man."

Dorothy was puzzled at this, for it sounded queer to hear a stuffed man speak, and to see him walk along beside her.

"Who are you?" asked the Scarecrow when he had stretched himself and yawned. "And where are you going?"

"My name is Dorothy," said the girl, "and I am going to the Emerald City, to ask the Great Oz to send me back to Kansas."

"Where is the Emerald City?" he inquired. "And who is Oz?"

"Why, don't you know?" she asked, in surprise.

"No, indeed—I don't know anything. You see, I am stuffed, so I have no brains at all," he answered her, sadly.

"Oh," said Dorothy, "I'm awfully sorry for you."

"Do you think," he asked, "if I go to the Emerald City with you, that the Great Oz would give me some brains?"

"I cannot tell," she returned, "but you may come with me, if you like. If Oz will not give you any brains you will be no worse off than you are now."

"That is true," said the Scarecrow. "You see," he continued confidentially, "I don't mind my legs and arms and body being stuffed, because I cannot get hurt. If anyone treads on my toes or sticks a pin into me, it doesn't matter, for I can't feel it. But I do not want people to call me a fool, and if my head stays stuffed with straw instead of with brains, how am I to know anything?"

"I understand how you feel," said the little girl,

who was truly sorry for him. "If you will come with me I'll ask Oz to do all he can for you."

"Thank you," he answered gratefully.

They walked back to the road. Dorothy helped him over the fence, and they started along the path of yellow brick.

Toto did not like this addition to the party at first. He smelled around the stuffed man as if he suspected there might be a nest of rats in the straw, and he often growled in a rather unfriendly way at the Scarecrow.

"Don't mind Toto," said Dorothy to her new friend. "He never bites."

"Oh, I'm not afraid," replied the Scarecrow. "He can't hurt the straw. Do let me carry that basket for you. I shall not mind it, for I can't get tired. I'll tell you a secret," he continued, as he walked along. "There is only one thing in the world I am afraid of."

"What is that?" asked Dorothy; "the Munchkin farmer who made you?"

"No," answered the Scarecrow; "it's fire."

After many hours of walking the light faded, and they found themselves stumbling along in the darkness. Dorothy could not see at all, but Toto could, and the Scarecrow declared he could see as well as by day. So she took hold of his arm and managed to get along fairly well.

"If you see any house, or any place where we can pass the night," she said, "you must tell me; for it is very uncomfortable walking in the dark."

Soon after the Scarecrow stopped. "I see a little cottage at the right of us," he said, "built of logs and branches. Shall we go there?"

"Yes, please," answered the child. "Indeed, I am all tired out."

So the Scarecrow led her through the trees until

131

they reached the cottage, and Dorothy entered and found a bed of dried leaves in one corner. She lay down at once, and with Toto beside her soon fell into a sound sleep. The Scarecrow, who was never tired, stood up in another corner and waited patiently until morning.

When Dorothy awoke the sun was shining through the trees and Toto had long been out chasing birds and squirrels. She sat up and looked around her. Scarecrow, still standing patiently in his corner, was waiting for her.

"We must go and search for water," she told him.

"Why do you want water?" he asked.

"To wash my face clean, and to drink, so the dry bread will not stick in my throat."

"It must be inconvenient to be made of flesh," said the Scarecrow, "for you must sleep, and eat, and drink. However, you have brains, and it is worth a lot of bother to be able to think properly."

They left the cottage and walked through the

trees until they found a little spring of clear water, where Dorothy drank and bathed and ate her breakfast. She saw there was not much bread left in the basket, and the girl was thankful the Scarecrow did not have to eat anything, for there was scarcely enough for herself and Toto for the day.

When she had finished her meal, and was about start walking again, she was startled to hear a deep groan nearby.

"What was that?" she asked timidly.

"I cannot imagine," replied the Scarecrow; "but we can go and see."

Just then another groan reached their ears, and it seemed to come from behind them. They turned and walked through the forest a few steps, when Dorothy discovered something shining in a ray of sunshine that fell between the trees. She ran to the place and then stopped short, with a cry of surprise.

One of the big trees had been partly chopped through, and standing beside it, with an uplifted ax in his hands, was a man made entirely of tin. His head and arms and legs were jointed upon his body, but he stood motionless, as if he could not stir at all.

Dorothy looked at him in amazement, and so did the Scarecrow, while Toto barked sharply and made a snap at the tin legs, which hurt his teeth.

"Did you groan?" asked Dorothy.

"Yes," answered the tin man, "I've been groaning for more than a year. No one has heard me before."

"What can I do for you?" she inquired softly, for she was moved by the sad voice in which he spoke.

"Get an oil-can and oil my joints," he answered. "They are rusted so that I cannot move them at all; if I am well oiled I shall soon be all right again. You will find an oil-can on a shelf in my cottage."

Dorothy at once ran back to the cottage and found the oil-can, and then she returned and asked anxiously, "Where are your joints?"

"Oil my neck, first," replied the Tin Woodman. So she oiled it, and as it was quite badly rusted the

Scarecrow took hold of the tin head and moved it gently from side to side until it worked freely, and then the man could turn it himself.

"Now oil the joints in my arms," he said. And Dorothy oiled them and the Scarecrow bent them carefully until they were as good as new.

The Tin Woodman gave a sigh of satisfaction and lowered his ax, leaning it against the tree. "This is a great comfort," he said. "I have been holding that ax in the air since I rusted. I'm glad to be able to put it down at last. Now, if you will oil the joints of my legs, I shall be all right once more."

So they oiled his legs until he could move them freely; and he thanked them again for his release. "I might have stood there always if you had not come along," he said; "so you have certainly saved my life. How did you happen to be here?"

"We are on our way to the Emerald City to see the Great Oz," she answered, "and we stopped at your cottage to pass the night."

"Why do you wish to see Oz?" he asked.

"I want him to send me back to Kansas, and the Scarecrow wants him to put a few brains into his head," she replied.

The Tin Woodman said, "Do you suppose Oz could give me a heart?"

"Why, I guess so," Dorothy answered. "It would be as easy as to give the Scarecrow brains."

"True," the Tin Woodman returned. "So, if you will allow me to join your party, I will also go to the Emerald City and ask Oz to help me."

"Come along," said the Scarecrow heartily, and Dorothy added that she would be pleased to have his company. So the Tin Woodman shouldered his ax and they all passed through the forest until they came to the road paved with yellow brick.

The Tin Woodman asked Dorothy to put the oil-can in her basket. "For," he said, "if I should get caught in the rain, I would need the oil-can badly."

It was a bit of good luck to have their new

comrade, for soon after they had begun their journey again they came to a place where the trees and branches grew so thick over the road that the travelers could not pass. But the Tin Woodman set to work with his ax and chopped so well that soon he cleared a passage for the entire party.

Dorothy was thinking so earnestly as they walked along that she did not notice when the Scarecrow stumbled into a hole. Indeed he was obliged to call to her to help him up again.

"Why didn't you walk around the hole?" asked the Tin Woodman.

"I don't know enough," replied the Scarecrow cheerfully. "My head is stuffed with straw, you know, and that is why I am going to Oz to ask him for some brains."

"Oh, I see," said the Tin Woodman. "But, after all, brains are not the best things in the world."

"Have you any?" inquired the Scarecrow.

"No, my head is quite empty," answered the Woodman. "But once I had brains, and a heart also; so, having tried them both, I should much rather have a heart."

"And why is that?" asked the Scarecrow.

"I will tell you my story, and then you will know."

So, while they were walking through the forest, the Tin Woodman told the following story:

"I was born the son of a woodman. When I grew up, I became a woodchopper too, and after my father died I took care of my old mother as long as she lived. Then I decided that instead of living alone I would marry, so that I might not be lonely.

"There was one of the Munchkin girls who was so beautiful that I soon grew to love her with all my heart. She, on her part, promised to marry me as soon as I could earn enough money to build a better house for her; so I set to work harder than ever. But the girl lived with an old woman who did not want her to marry, for she was so lazy she wished the girl to remain with her and do the housework. So the old woman went to the Wicked Witch of the East, and promised her two sheep if she would prevent the marriage. The Wicked Witch enchanted my ax, and when I was chopping away at my best one day, for I was anxious to get the new house and my wife as soon as possible, the ax slipped all at once and cut off my left leg.

"This at first seemed a great misfortune, for I knew a one-legged man could not do very well as a woodchopper. So I went to a tinsmith and had him

139

make me a new leg out of tin. The leg worked very well, once I was used to it. But when I began chopping again, my ax slipped and cut off my right leg. Again I went to the tinsmith, and again he made me a leg out of tin.

"After this the enchanted ax cut off my arms, one after the other; but I had them replaced with tin ones. The Wicked Witch then made the ax slip and cut off my head, and at first I thought that was the end of me. But the tinsmith happened to come along, and he made me a new head out of tin.

"I thought I had beaten the Wicked Witch then, and I worked harder than ever; but I little knew how cruel my enemy could be. She thought of a new way to kill my love for the beautiful Munchkin maiden, and made my ax slip again, so that it cut right through my body, splitting me into two halves. Once more the tinsmith came to my help and made me a body of tin, fastening my tin arms and legs and head to it, by means of joints, so that I could move around as well as ever. But, alas! I had now no heart, so that I lost all my love for the Munchkin girl. I suppose she is still living with the old woman, waiting for me to come after her.

"It did not matter any more if my ax slipped, for it could no longer cut me. There was only one danger—that my joints would rust; but I kept an oil-can in my cottage and took care to oil myself whenever I needed it. However, there came a day when I forgot to do this, and, being caught in a rainstorm, my joints rusted, and I was left to stand in the woods until you came to help me. During the year I stood there I had time to think that the greatest loss I had known was the loss of my heart. While I was in love I was the happiest man on earth; but no one can love who has not a heart, and so I am resolved to ask Oz to give me one. If he does, I will go back to the Munchkin maiden and marry her."

Both Dorothy and the Scarecrow had been

greatly interested in the story of the Tin Woodman, and now they knew why he was so anxious to get a new heart. "All the same," said the Scarecrow, "I shall ask for brains; for a fool would not know what to do with a heart if he had one."

"I shall take the heart," returned the Tin Woodman; "for brains do not make one happy, and happiness is the best thing in the world."

Dorothy did not say anything, for she was puzzled to know which of her two friends was right. What worried her most was that the bread was nearly gone, and another meal for herself and Toto would empty the basket.

All this time Dorothy and her companions had been walking through the thick woods. The road was still paved with yellow brick, but these were much covered by dried branches and dead leaves from the trees, and the walking was not at all good.

There were few birds in this part of the forest, but now and then there came a deep growl from some wild animal hidden among the trees. These sounds made the little girl's heart beat fast, for she did not know what made them; but Toto knew, and he walked close to Dorothy's side, and did not even bark in return.

"How long will it be," the child asked of the Tin Woodman, "before we are out of the forest?"

"I cannot tell," was the answer, "for I have never been to the Emerald City. But my father went there once, when I was a boy, and he said it was a long journey through a dangerous country, although nearer to the city where Oz dwells the country is beautiful. But I am not afraid so long as I have my oil-can, and nothing can hurt the Scarecrow, while you have been kissed by the Good Witch, and that will protect you from harm."

"But Toto!" said the girl anxiously. "What will protect him?"

"We must protect him ourselves if he is in danger," replied the Tin Woodman.

Just as he spoke there came from the forest a terrible roar, and the next moment a great Lion bounded into the road. With a blow of his paw he sent the Scarecrow spinning over to the edge of the road, and then he struck at the Tin Woodman with his sharp claws. But, to the Lion's surprise, he could make no impression on the tin, although the Woodman fell over in the road and lay still.

Little Toto ran barking toward the Lion, and the great beast had opened his mouth to bite the dog, when Dorothy, fearing Toto would be killed, and heedless of danger, rushed forward, and slapped the Lion upon his nose as hard as she could, crying out: "Don't you dare to bite Toto! You ought to be ashamed of yourself, a big beast like you, to bite a poor little dog!"

"I didn't bite him," said the Lion, as he rubbed his nose with his paw where Dorothy had hit it.

"No, but you tried to," she retorted. "You are nothing but a big coward."

"I know it," said the Lion, hanging his head in shame. "But how can I help it?"

"I don't know, I'm sure. To think of your striking a stuffed man, like the poor Scarecrow!"

"Is he stuffed?" asked the Lion in surprise, as he watched her pick up the Scarecrow and set him upon his feet, while she patted him into shape.

"Of course he's stuffed," replied Dorothy, who was still angry.

"That's why he went over so easily," remarked the

Lion. "It astonished me to see him whirl around so. Is the other one stuffed also?"

"No," said Dorothy, "he's made of tin." And she helped the Woodman up again.

"That's why he nearly blunted my claws," said the Lion. "When they scratched against the tin it made a cold shiver run down my back. What is that little animal you are so tender of?"

"He is my dog, Toto," answered Dorothy.

"Is he made of tin, or stuffed?" asked the Lion.

"Neither. He's a—a meat dog," said the girl.

"Oh! He's a curious animal and seems remarkably small, now that I look at him. No one would think of biting such a little thing, except a coward like me," continued the Lion sadly.

"What makes you a coward?" asked Dorothy.

"It's a mystery," replied the Lion. "All the other animals in the forest naturally expect me to be brave. I learned that if I roared very loudly every living thing was frightened and got out of my way.

Whenever I've met a man I've been awfully scared; but I just roared at him, and he has always run away. If the elephants and the tigers and the bears had ever tried to fight me, I should have run myself; but as soon as they hear me roar they try to get away from me, and of course I let them go."

"But that isn't right. The "king of beasts" shouldn't be a coward," said the Scarecrow.

"I know," returned the Lion, wiping a tear from his eye with the tip of his tail. "It is my great sorrow, and makes my life very unhappy. But whenever there is danger, my heart begins to beat fast."

"Perhaps you have heart disease," suggested the Tin Woodman.

"It may be," said the Lion.

"If you have," continued the Tin Woodman, "it proves you have a heart. I have no heart."

"Perhaps," said the Lion thoughtfully, "if I had no heart I should not be a coward."

"Have you brains?" asked the Scarecrow.

"I suppose so. I've never looked to see," replied the Lion.

"I am going to the Great Oz to ask him to give me some," remarked the Scarecrow.

"And I am going to ask him to give me a heart," said the Woodman.

"And I am going to ask him to send Toto and me back to Kansas," added Dorothy.

"Do you think Oz could give me courage?" asked the Cowardly Lion.

"Just as easily as he could give me brains," said the Scarecrow.

"Or give me a heart," said the Tin Woodman.

"Or send me back to Kansas," said Dorothy.

"Then, if you don't mind, I'll go with you," said the Lion, "for my life is simply unbearable without a bit of courage."

"You will be very welcome," answered Dorothy, "for you will help to keep away the other wild beasts. It seems to me they must be more cowardly than you are if they allow you to scare them."

"They really are," said the Lion, "but that doesn't make me any braver, and as long as I know myself to be a coward I shall be unhappy."

So once more the little company set off upon the journey, the Lion walking with stately strides at Dorothy's side. Toto did not approve of this new comrade at first, for he could not forget how nearly he had been crushed between the Lion's great jaws. But after a time he became more at ease, and presently Toto and the Cowardly Lion had grown to be good friends.

# SECRETS
# REVEALED

# Down the Rabbit-hole

From *Alice's Adventures in Wonderland*
by Lewis Carroll

Alice was beginning to get very tired of sitting by her sister on the bank, and of having nothing to do. Once or twice she had peeped into the book her sister was reading, but it had no pictures or conversations in it. "And what is the use of a book," thought Alice, "without pictures or conversation?"

So she was considering (as well as she could, for the hot day made her feel very sleepy and stupid) whether the pleasure of making a daisy chain would be worth the trouble of getting up and picking the

152

daisies, when suddenly a White Rabbit with pink eyes ran close by her.

There was nothing so very remarkable in that. Nor did Alice think it so very much out of the way to hear the Rabbit say to itself, "Oh dear! Oh dear! I shall be late!" (When she thought it over afterward, it occurred to her that she ought to have wondered at this, but at the time it all seemed quite natural.) When the Rabbit actually took a watch out of its waistcoat-pocket, looked at it, and then hurried on, Alice started to her feet, for it flashed across her mind that she had never seen a rabbit with either a waistcoat-pocket or a watch to take out of it. Burning with curiosity, she ran across the field after it, and fortunately was just in time to see it pop down a large rabbit-hole under the hedge.

In another moment down went Alice after it. The rabbit-hole went straight on like a tunnel for some way, and then dipped suddenly down, so that Alice had not a moment to think about stopping herself before she found herself falling down a well.

First, she tried to look down and make out what she was coming to, but it was too dark to see anything. Then she looked at the sides of the well, and she noticed that they were filled with cupboards and bookshelves. Here and there she saw maps and pictures hung upon pegs. She took down a jar from one of the shelves as she passed. It was labeled orange marmalade, but to her great disappointment it was empty. She did not like to drop the jar for fear of killing somebody, so managed to put it into one of the cupboards as she fell past it.

"Well!" thought Alice to herself. "After such a fall as this, I shall think nothing of tumbling down stairs! How brave they'll all think me at home! Why, I wouldn't say anything about it, even if I fell off the top of the house!"

Down, down, down. Would the fall never come to an end? "I wonder how many miles I've fallen by

this time?" she said aloud. "I must be getting somewhere near the center of the earth. Let me see, that would be four thousand miles down, I think…" (For, you see, Alice had learned several things of this sort in her lessons in the schoolroom, and though this was not a very good opportunity for showing off her knowledge, as there was no one to listen to her, still it was good practice to say it over.)

"Yes, that's about the right distance—but then I wonder what latitude or longitude I've got to?" (Alice had no idea what latitude was, or longitude either, but thought they were nice grand words to say.)

Presently she began again. "I wonder if I shall fall right through the earth! How funny it'll seem to come out among the people that walk with their heads downward! But I shall have to ask them what the name of the country is, you know. Please, Ma'am, is this New Zealand or Australia?" (And she tried to curtsey as she spoke—fancy curtseying as you're falling through the air! Do you think you could manage it?) "And what an ignorant little girl she'll think me for asking! No, it'll never do to ask, but perhaps I shall see it written up somewhere."

Down, down, down. There was nothing else to do, so Alice soon began talking again. "Dinah'll miss me very much tonight, I should think!" (Dinah was the cat.) "I hope they'll remember her saucer of milk at tea-time. Dinah my dear! I wish you were down here with me! There are no mice in the air, I'm afraid, but you might catch a bat, and that's very like a mouse, you know. But do cats eat bats, I wonder?"

Alice began to get rather sleepy, and went on saying to herself, in a dreamy sort of way, "Do cats eat bats?" and sometimes, "Do bats eat cats?" (For, you see, as she couldn't answer either question, it didn't much matter which way she put it.)

She felt that she was dozing off, and had just begun to dream that she was walking hand in hand with Dinah, and saying to her earnestly, "Now, Dinah, tell me the truth: did you ever eat a bat?" when suddenly, *thump!* Down she came upon a heap of sticks and dry leaves, and the fall was over.

Alice was not a bit hurt, and she jumped up on to her feet in a moment. She looked up, but it was all dark overhead. Before her was another long passage, and the White Rabbit was still in sight, hurrying down it. There was not a moment to be lost: away went Alice like the wind, and was just in time to hear it say, as it turned a corner, "Oh my ears and whiskers, how late it's getting!"

She was close behind it when she turned the corner, but the Rabbit was no longer to be seen. She found herself in a long, low hall, which was lit up by a row of lamps hanging from the roof.

There were doors all around the hall, but they were all locked, and when Alice had been all the way down one side and up the other, trying every door, she walked sadly down the middle, wondering how she was ever to get out again…

# The Terrible Secret

From *The Railway Children*
by E. Nesbit

*Roberta (Bobbie), Peter, and Phyllis have to move to the country with
their mother when their father is suddenly taken away. The children
spend much of their time watching the trains that pass by their cottage.*

When they first went to live at Three Chimneys,
the children had talked a great deal about
their Father, and had asked a great many questions
about him, and what he was doing and where he
was and when he would come home. Mother always
answered their questions as well as she could. But
as the time went on they grew to speak less of him.

# The Terrible Secret

Bobbie had felt almost from the first that for some strange miserable reason these questions hurt Mother and made her sad. And little by little the others came to have this feeling, too, though they could not have put it into words.

One day, when Mother was working so hard that she could not leave off even for ten minutes, Bobbie carried up her tea to the big bare room that they called Mother's workshop. It had hardly any furniture. Just a table and a chair and a rug. But always big pots of flowers on the windowsills and on the mantelpiece. The children saw to that. And from the three long uncurtained windows the beautiful stretch of meadow and moorland, the far violet of the hills, and the unchanging changefulness of cloud and sky.

"Here's your tea, Mother-love," said Bobbie. "Do drink it while it's hot."

Mother laid down her pen among the pages that were scattered all over the table, pages covered with her writing, which was almost as plain as print, and much prettier. She ran her hands into her hair, as if she were going to pull it out by handfuls.

"Poor dear head," said Bobbie, "does it ache?"

"No—yes—not much," said Mother. "Bobbie, do you think Peter and Phil are forgetting Father?"

"No," said Bobbie, indignantly. "Why?"

"None of you ever speak of him now."

Bobbie stood first on one leg and then on the other as she thought how to reply.

"We often talk about him when we're by ourselves," she said.

"But not to me," said Mother. "Why?"

Bobbie did not find it easy to say why. "I— you—" she said and stopped. She went over to the window and looked out.

"Bobbie, come here," said her Mother, and Bobbie came.

"Now," said Mother with a gentle smile, putting her arm round Bobbie and laying her ruffled head against Bobbie's shoulder, "do try to tell me, dear."

Bobbie fidgeted.

"Tell Mother."

"Well, then," said Bobbie, "I thought you were so unhappy about Daddy not being here, it made you worse when I talked about him. So I stopped."

"And the others?"

"I don't know about the others," said Bobbie. "I never said anything about that to them. But I expect they felt the same about it as me."

"Bobbie dear," said Mother, still leaning her head against her, "I'll tell you. Besides parting from Father, he and I have had a great sorrow—oh, terrible—worse than anything you can think of, and at first it did hurt to hear you all talking of him as if everything were just the same. But it would be much more terrible if you were to forget him. That would be worse than anything."

"The trouble," said Bobbie, in a very little voice, "I promised I would never ask you any questions, and I never have, have I? But—the trouble—it won't last always?"

"No," said Mother, "the worst will be over when Father comes home to us."

"I wish I could comfort you," said Bobbie.

"Oh, my dear, do you suppose you don't? Do you think I haven't noticed how good you've all been, not quarreling nearly as much as you used to—and all the little kind things you do for me—the flowers, and cleaning my shoes, and tearing up to make my bed before I get time to do it myself?"

Bobbie had sometimes wondered whether Mother noticed these things.

"That's nothing," she said, "to what—"

"I must get on with my work," said Mother, giving Bobbie one last squeeze. "Don't say anything to the others."

That evening in the hour before bedtime instead of reading to the children Mother told them stories of the games she and Father used to have when they were children and lived near each other in the country—tales of the adventures of Father with Mother's brothers when they were all boys together. Very funny stories they were, and the children laughed as they listened.

"Uncle Edward died before he was grown up, didn't he?" said Phyllis, as Mother lighted the bedroom candles.

"Yes, dear," said Mother, "you would have loved him. He was such a brave boy, and so adventurous. Always in mischief, and yet friends with everybody in spite of it. And your Uncle Reggie's in Ceylon, and Father's away, too. But I think they'd all like to think we'd enjoyed talking about the things they used to do. Don't you think so?"

"Not Uncle Edward," said Phyllis, in a shocked tone, "he's in heaven."

"You don't suppose he's forgotten us and all the old times, because God has taken him, any more than I forget him. Oh, no, he remembers. He's only away for a little time. We shall see him some day."

"And Uncle Reggie—and Father, too?" said Peter, softly.

"Yes," said Mother. "Uncle Reggie and Father, too. Good night, my darlings."

"Good night," said everyone. When it was her turn, Bobbie hugged her mother more closely even than usual, and whispered in her ear, "Oh, I do love you so, Mummy—I do—I do—"

When Bobbie came to think it all over, she tried not to wonder what the great trouble was. But she could not always help it. Father was not dead—like poor Uncle Edward—Mother had said so. And he was not ill, or Mother would have been with him. Being poor wasn't the trouble. Bobbie knew it was something nearer the heart than money could be.

"I mustn't try to think what it is," she told herself, "no, I mustn't. I am glad Mother noticed about us not quarreling so much. We'll keep that up." But alas, that very afternoon she and Peter had what Peter called a first-class shindy.

They had not been a week at Three Chimneys before they had asked Mother to let them have a piece of garden each for their very own, and she had agreed, and the south border under the peach trees had been divided into three pieces and they were allowed to plant whatever they liked there.

Phyllis had planted mignonette and nasturtium

and Virginia Stock in hers. The seeds came up, and though they looked just like weeds, Phyllis believed that they would bear flowers some day. The Virginia Stock justified her faith quite soon, and her garden was bright with a band of vivid little flowers, pink and white and red and mauve.

"I can't weed for fear I pull up the wrong things," she used to say comfortably, "it saves a lot of work."

Peter sowed vegetable seeds in his—carrots and onions and turnips. The seed was given to him by the farmer who lived in the nice black-and-white, wood-and-plaster house just beyond the bridge. He kept turkeys and guinea fowls, and was a most amiable man. But Peter's vegetables never had much of a chance, because he liked to use the earth of his garden for digging canals, and making forts and earthworks for his toy soldiers. And the seeds of vegetables rarely come to much in a soil that is constantly being disturbed for the purposes of war and irrigation.

# The Terrible Secret

Bobbie planted rose-bushes in her garden, but all the little new leaves of the rose-bushes shriveled and withered, perhaps because she moved them from the other part of the garden in May, which is not at all the right time of year for moving roses. But she would not own that they were dead, until the day when Perks came up to see the garden, and told her quite plainly that all her roses were as dead as doornails.

"They're only good for bonfires, Miss," he said. "You just dig 'em up and burn 'em, and I'll give you some nice fresh roots outer my garden—pansies, and stocks, and sweet willies, and forget-me-nots. I'll bring 'em all along tomorrow if you get the ground ready."

So next day she set to work, and that happened to be the day when Mother had praised her and the others about not quarreling. She moved the rose-bushes and carried them to the other end of the garden, where the rubbish heap was that they

planned to make into a bonfire of when Guy
Fawkes' Day came.

Meanwhile Peter had decided to flatten out all
his forts and earthworks, with a view to making a
model of the railway-tunnel, cutting, embankment,
canal, aqueduct, bridges, and all.

So when Bobbie came back from her last thorny
journey with the dead rose-bushes, he had got the
rake and was using it busily.

"I was using the rake," said Bobbie.

"Well, I'm using it now," said Peter.

"But I had it first," said Bobbie.

"Then it's my turn now," said Peter.
And that was how the quarrel began.
"You're always being disagreeable
about nothing," said Peter, after some
heated argument.

"I had the rake first," said Bobbie,
flushed and defiant, holding onto
its handle.

"Don't—I tell you I said this morning I meant to have it. Didn't I, Phil?"

Phyllis said she didn't want to be mixed up in their rows. And instantly, of course, she was.

"If you remember, you ought to say."

"Of course she doesn't remember—but she might say so."

"I wish I'd had a brother instead of two whiny little kiddy sisters," said Peter. This was always recognized as indicating the high-water mark of Peter's rage.

Bobbie made the reply she always made to it.

"I can't think why little boys were ever invented," and just as she said it she

looked up, and saw the three long windows of
Mother's workshop flashing in the red rays of the
sun. The sight brought back those words of praise:
"You don't quarrel like you used to do."

"Oh!" cried Bobbie, just as if she had been hit, or
had caught her finger in a door, or had felt the
hideous sharp beginnings of toothache.

"What's the matter?" said Phyllis.

Bobbie wanted to say:"Don't let's quarrel.
Mother hates it so," but she couldn't. Peter was
looking too disagreeable and insulting.

"Take the horrid rake, then," was the best she
could manage. And she suddenly let go her hold on
the handle. Peter had been holding on to it too
firmly, and now that the pull the other way was
suddenly stopped, he staggered and fell over
backward, the teeth of the rake between his feet.

"Serve you right," said Bobbie, before she could
stop herself.

Peter lay still for half a moment—long enough to

frighten Bobbie a little. Then he frightened her a little more, for he sat up, screamed once, turned rather pale, and then lay back and began to shriek, faintly but steadily. It sounded exactly like a pig being killed a quarter of a mile off.

Mother put her head out of the window, and it wasn't half a minute after that she was in the garden kneeling by the side of Peter, who never for an instant ceased to squeal.

"What happened, Bobbie?" Mother asked.

"It was because of the rake," said Phyllis. "Peter was pulling at it, so was Bobbie, and she let go and he went over."

"Stop that noise, Peter," said Mother. "Come. Stop at once."

Peter used up what breath he had left in a last squeal and stopped.

"Now," said Mother, "are you hurt?"

"He must be really hurt, or he wouldn't make such a fuss," said Bobbie, still trembling with fury but feeling scared, "he's not a coward!"

"I think my foot's broken off, that's all," said Peter, huffily, and sat up. Then he turned quite white. Mother put her arm around him.

"He is hurt," she said, "he's fainted. Here, Bobbie, sit down and take his head on your lap."

Then Mother undid Peter's boots. As she took the right one off, red blood dripped from his foot on to the ground. And when the stocking came off there were three red wounds in Peter's foot and ankle, where the teeth of the rake had bitten him, and his foot was covered with red smears.

"Run for water—a basinful," said Mother, and Phyllis ran. She upset most of the water out of the basin in her haste, and had to fetch more in a jug.

Peter did not open his eyes again till Mother had tied her handkerchief round his foot, and she and Bobbie had carried him in and laid him on the brown wooden settle in the dining room. By this time Phyllis was halfway to the Doctor's.

Mother sat by Peter and bathed his foot and talked to him, and Bobbie went out and got tea ready, and put on the kettle.

"It's all I can do," she thought to herself. "Oh, suppose Peter should die, or be a helpless cripple for life, or have to walk with crutches, or wear a boot with a sole like a log of wood!" She stood by the back door reflecting on these gloomy possibilities, her eyes fixed on the water-butt.

"I wish I'd never been born," she said, and she said it out loud.

The Doctor came and looked at the foot and bandaged it beautifully, and said that Peter must not put it to the ground for at least a week.

"He won't be lame, or have to wear crutches or have a lump on his foot, will he?" whispered Bobbie, breathlessly, at the door.

"My aunt! No!" said Dr. Forrest, "he'll be as nimble as ever on his pins in a fortnight. Don't you worry, little Mother Goose."

It was when Mother had gone to the gate with the Doctor to take his last instructions and Phyllis was filling the kettle for tea, that Peter and Bobbie found themselves alone.

"He says you won't be lame," said Bobbie.

"Oh, course I shan't, silly," said Peter, very much relieved all the same.

"Oh, Peter, I am sorry," said Bobbie, after a pause.

"That's all right," said Peter, gruffly.

"It was all my fault," said Bobbie.

"Rot," said Peter.

"If we hadn't quarreled, it wouldn't have happened. I knew it was wrong to quarrel. I wanted to say so, but somehow I couldn't."

"Don't drivel," said Peter. "I shouldn't have stopped if you had said it. Not likely."

"But I knew it was wrong to quarrel," said Bobbie, in tears, "and now you're hurt and—"

"Now look here," said Peter, firmly, "you just dry up. If you're not careful, you'll turn into a beastly little Sunday-school prig, so I tell you."

"I don't mean to be a prig. But it's so hard not to be when you're really trying to be good."

"Not it," said Peter, "it's a jolly good thing it wasn't you that was hurt. I'm glad it was me. There! If it had been you, you'd have been lying on the sofa looking like a suffering angel and being the light of the anxious household and all that. And I couldn't have stood it."

"No, I shouldn't," said Bobbie.

"Yes, you would," said Peter.

"I tell you I shouldn't."

"I tell you you would."

"Oh, children," said Mother's voice at the door.

"Quarreling again? Already?"

"We aren't quarreling—not really," said Peter. "I wish you wouldn't think it's rows every time we don't agree!"

When Mother had gone out again, Bobbie broke out, "Peter, I am sorry you're hurt. But you are a beast to say I'm a prig."

"Well," said Peter unexpectedly, "perhaps I am. You did say I wasn't a coward, even when you were in such a wax. The only thing is—don't you be a prig, that's all. You keep your eyes open and if you feel priggishness coming on just stop in time. See?"

"Yes," said Bobbie, "I see."

"Then let's call it Pax," said Peter, magnanimously. "Bury the hatchet. I say, Bobbie, old chap, I am tired."

At first Bobbie found it quite hard to be as nice to him as she wanted to be, for fear he should think her priggish. But that soon wore off, and both she and Phyllis were, as he observed, jolly good sorts.

Mother sat with him when his sisters were out. And the words, "he's not a coward," made Peter determined not to fuss about the pain in his foot, though it was rather bad. Praise helps people very much, sometimes.

There were visitors, too. Mrs. Perks came up to ask how he was, and so did the Station Master, and several of the village people. But the time went slowly, slowly.

"I do wish there was something to read," said Peter. "I've read all our books fifty times over."

"I'll go to the Doctor's," said Phyllis, "he's sure to have some."

"Only about how to be ill, and about people's nasty insides, I expect," said Peter.

"Perks has a whole heap of magazines that came out of trains when people are tired of them," said Bobbie. "I'll run down and ask him." So the girls went their two ways.

Bobbie found Perks busy cleaning lamps. "And

how's the young gent?" he asked.

"Better, thanks," said Bobbie, "but he's most frightfully bored. I came to ask if you'd got any magazines you could lend him."

"There, now," said Perks, regretfully, "why didn't I think of that? I was trying to think of something as 'ud amuse him only this morning, and I couldn't think of anything better than a guinea-pig. And a young chap I know's going to fetch that over for him this teatime."

"How lovely! A real live guinea! He will be pleased. But he'd like the magazines as well."

"That's just it," said Perks. "I've sent the pick of 'em to Snigson's boy—him what's just getting over the pewmonia. But I've lots of illustrated papers."

He turned to the pile of papers in the corner and took up a heap six inches thick.

"There!" he said. "I'll just slip a bit of string and a bit of paper round 'em."

He pulled an old newspaper from the pile and

spread it on the table, and made a neat parcel of it.

"There," said he, "there's lots of pictures, and if he likes to mess 'em about with his paint-box, or colored chalks or what not, why, let him. I don't want 'em."

"You're a dear," said Bobbie. She took the parcel and set off for home. The papers were heavy, and when she had to wait at the level-crossing while a train went by, she rested the parcel on the top of the gate. And idly she looked at the printing on the paper that the parcel was wrapped in.

Suddenly she clutched the parcel tighter and bent her head over it. It seemed like some horrible dream. She read on—the bottom of the column was torn off—she could read no farther.

She never remembered how she got home. But she went on tiptoe to her room and locked the door. Then she undid the parcel and read that column again, sitting on the edge of her bed. When she had read all there was, she drew a long breath.

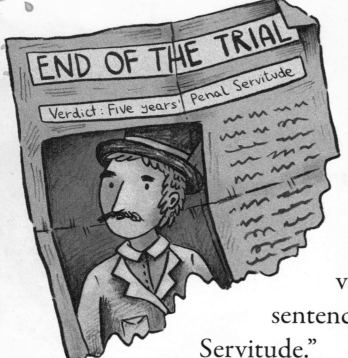

"So now I know," she said. What she had read was headed, "End of the Trial. Verdict. Sentence."

The name of the man who had been tried was the name of her Father. The verdict was "Guilty." And the sentence was "Five years' Penal Servitude."

"Oh, Daddy," she whispered, crushing the paper hard, "it's not true—I don't believe it. You never did it! Never, never, never!"

There was a hammering on the door.

"What is it?" said Bobbie.

"It's me," said the voice of Phyllis; "it's time for tea, and a boy's brought Peter a guinea-pig. Come along down."

And Bobbie had to.

# The Banquet Lamp

From *Rebecca of Sunnybrook Farm*
by Kate Douglas Wiggin

*Rebecca is sent to live with her two unmarried aunts.*
*She and her friends have been selling soap in order to try and*
*win the "banquet lamp"—a tall elaborate table lamp—that the*
*soap company are giving away as a reward for sales.*

There had been company at the brick house
to the bountiful Thanksgiving dinner that
had been provided at one o'clock—the Burnham
sisters, who lived between North Riverboro and
Shaker Village, and who for more than a quarter of
a century had come to pass the vacation with the

Sawyers every year. Rebecca sat silent with a book after the dinner dishes were washed, and after what felt like many hours—when it was nearly five—asked if she might go to the Simpsons'.

"What do you want to run after those Simpson children for on a Thanksgiving Day?" queried Miss Miranda. "Can't you set still for once and listen to the improvin' conversation of your elders? You never can let well enough alone, but want to be forever on the move."

"The Simpsons have a new lamp, and Emma Jane and I promised to go up and see it lighted, and make it a kind of a party."

"What under the canopy did they want of a lamp, and where did they get the money to pay for it? If Abner was at home, I should think he'd been swappin' again," said Miss Miranda.

"The children got it as a prize for selling soap," replied Rebecca. "They've been working for a year, and you know I told you that Emma Jane and I helped them the Saturday afternoon you were in Portland."

"I didn't take notice, I s'pose, for it's the first time I ever heard the lamp mentioned. Well, you can go for an hour, and no more. Remember it's as dark at six as it is at midnight. Would you like to take along some Baldwin apples? And what have you got in the pocket of that new dress that is making it sag down so?"

"It's my nuts and raisins from dinner," replied Rebecca, who never succeeded in keeping the most innocent action a secret from her aunt Miranda. "They're just what you gave me on my plate."

"Why didn't you eat them?"

"Because I'd had enough dinner, and I thought if I saved these, it would make the Simpsons' party better," stammered Rebecca, who hated to be scolded and examined before company.

"They were your own, Rebecca," interposed aunt Jane, "and if you chose to save them to give away, it is all right. We ought never to let this day pass without giving our neighbors something to be thankful for, instead of taking all the time to think of our own mercies."

The Burnham sisters nodded approvingly as Rebecca went out, and remarked that they had never seen a child grow and improve so fast in so short a time.

"There's plenty of room left for more improvement, as you'd know if she lived in the same house with you," answered Miranda. "She's into every namable thing in the neighborhood, an' not only into it, but generally at the head an' front of it—especially when it's mischief. Of all the foolishness I ever heard of, that lamp beats everything; it's just like those Simpsons, but I didn't suppose any of those children had brains enough to sell anything."

"One of them must have," said Miss Ellen Burnham, "for the girl that was selling soap at the

Ladds' in North Riverboro was described by Adam Ladd as the most remarkable and winning child he ever saw."

"It must have been Clara Belle, and I should never call her remarkable," answered Miss Miranda. "Has Adam been home again?"

"Yes, he's been staying a few days with his aunt. There's no limit to the money he's making, they say; and he always brings presents for all the neighbors. This time it was a full set of furs for Mrs. Ladd—and to think we can remember the time he was a barefoot boy without two shirts to his back! It is strange he hasn't married, with all his money, and him so fond of children that he always has a pack of them at his heels."

"There's hope for him still, though," said Miss Jane smilingly. "I don't s'pose he can be more than thirty."

"He could get a wife in Riverboro if he was a hundred and thirty," remarked Miss Miranda.

187

"Adam's aunt says he was so taken with the little girl that sold the soap—Clara Belle, did you say her name was?—that he declared he was going to bring her a Christmas present," continued Miss Ellen.

"Well, there's no accountin' for tastes," exclaimed Miss Miranda. "Clara Belle's got cross-eyes and red hair, but I'd be the last one to grudge her a Christmas present—the more Adam Ladd gives to her the less the town'll have to."

"Isn't there another Simpson girl?" asked Miss Lydia Burnham. "For this one couldn't have been cross-eyed—I remember Mrs. Ladd saying Adam remarked about this child's handsome eyes. He said it was her eyes that made him buy the three hundred cakes. Mrs. Ladd has it stacked up in the shed chamber."

"Three hundred cakes!" cried Miranda. "Well, as always, there's one crop for sure that never fails in Riverboro!"

"What's that?" asked Miss Lydia politely.

# The Banquet Lamp

"The fool crop," responded Miranda tersely, and changed the subject, much to Jane's gratitude, for she had been nervous and ill at ease for the last fifteen minutes. What child in Riverboro could be described as remarkable and winning, save Rebecca? What child had wonderful eyes, except the same Rebecca? And finally, was there ever a child in the world who could make a man buy soap by the hundred cakes, save Rebecca?

Meantime the "remarkable" child had flown up the road in the deepening dusk, but she had not gone far before she heard the sound of hurrying footsteps, and saw a well-known figure coming in her direction. In a moment she and Emma Jane met and exchanged a breathless embrace.

"Something awful has happened with the lamp," panted Emma Jane.

"Don't tell me it's broken," exclaimed Rebecca.

"No! Oh, no! Not that! It was packed in straw, and every piece came out all right; and I was there. And I never said a single thing about your selling the three hundred cakes that got the lamp, so that we could be together when you told."

"Our selling the three hundred cakes," corrected Rebecca; "You did as much as I."

"No, I didn't, Rebecca Randall. I just sat at the gate and held the horse."

"Yes, but whose horse was it that took us to North Riverboro? And besides, it just happened to be my turn. If you had gone in and found Mr. Aladdin you would have had the wonderful lamp given to you. But what's the trouble?"

"The Simpsons have no kerosene and no wicks. I guess they thought a banquet lamp was something that lighted itself, and burned without any help.

Seesaw has gone to the doctor's to try if he can borrow a wick, and mother let me have a pint of oil, but she says she won't give me any more. We never even thought of the expense of keeping up the lamp, Rebecca."

"No, we didn't, but let's not worry about that till after the party. I have a handful of nuts and raisins and some apples."

"I have peppermints and maple sugar," said Emma Jane. "They had a real Thanksgiving dinner; the doctor gave them sweet potatoes and cranberries and turnips; father sent a spare-rib, and Mrs. Cobb a chicken and a jar of mincemeat."

At half past five one might have looked in at the Simpsons' windows, and seen the party at its height. Mrs. Simpson had let the kitchen fire die out, and had brought the baby to grace the festive scene. The lamp seemed to be having the party, and receiving the guests. The children had taken the one small table in the house, and it was placed in the far corner of the room to serve as a pedestal. On it stood the sacred, the adored, the long-desired object; almost as beautiful, and nearly half as large as the advertisement. The brass glistened like gold, and the crimson paper shade glowed like a giant ruby. In the wide splash of light that it flung upon the floor sat the Simpsons, in reverent and solemn silence, Emma Jane standing behind them, hand in hand with Rebecca. There seemed to be no desire for conversation—the occasion was too thrilling and serious for that. The lamp, it was tacitly felt by everybody, was dignifying the party, and providing sufficient entertainment simply by its presence; being fully as satisfactory in its way as a pianola or a string band.

"I wish that father could see it," whispered Clara Belle loyally.

"If he onth thaw it he'd want to thwap it," murmured Susan sagaciously.

At the appointed hour Rebecca dragged herself reluctantly away from the enchanting scene.

"I'll turn the lamp out the minute I think you and Emma Jane are home," said Clara Belle. "And I'm so glad you both live where you can see it shine. I wonder how long it will burn without bein' filled if I only keep it lit one hour every night?"

"You needn't put it out for want o' kerosene,"

said Seesaw, coming in from the shed, "for there's a great keg of it settin' out there. Mr. Tubbs brought it over from North Riverboro and said somebody sent an order by mail for it."

Rebecca squeezed Emma Jane's arm, and Emma Jane gave a rapturous return squeeze.

"It was Mr. Aladdin," whispered Rebecca, as they ran down the path to the gate.

Rebecca entered the home dining room joyously. The Burnham sisters had gone and the two aunts were knitting.

"It was a heavenly party," she cried, taking off her hat and cape.

"Go back and see if you have shut the door tight, and then lock it," said Miss Miranda, in her usual austere manner.

"It was a heavenly party," reiterated Rebecca, coming in again, much too excited to be easily crushed. "And oh! Aunt Jane, Aunt Miranda, if you'll come into the kitchen and look out of the sink window, you can see the banquet lamp shining all red, just as if the Simpsons' house was on fire."

"And probably it will be before long," observed Miranda. "I've got no patience with such foolish goin's on."

Jane accompanied Rebecca into the kitchen. Although the glimmer that she was able to see from that distance did not seem to her a dazzling exhibition, she tried to be enthusiastic.

"Rebecca, who was it that sold the three hundred cakes of soap to Mr. Ladd in North Riverboro?"

"Mr. Who?" exclaimed Rebecca

"Mr. Ladd, in North Riverboro."

"Is that his real name?" queried Rebecca in astonishment. "I didn't make a bad guess," and she laughed softly to herself.

"I asked you who sold the soap to Adam Ladd?" resumed Miss Jane.

"Adam Ladd! then he's "A. Ladd"—what fun!"

"Answer me, Rebecca."

"Oh! excuse me, aunt Jane, I was busy thinking. Emma Jane and I sold the soap to Mr. Ladd."

"Did you tease him, or make him buy it?"

"Now, aunt Jane, how could I make a big grown-up man buy anything if he didn't want to? He needed the soap dreadfully he said, as a present for his aunt."

Miss Jane still looked a little unconvinced, though she only said, "I hope your aunt Miranda won't mind, but you know how particular she is, Rebecca, and I really wish you wouldn't do anything out of the ordinary without asking her first, for your actions are very strange."

"There can't be anything wrong this time," Rebecca answered confidently. "Emma Jane sold her cakes to her own relations and to uncle Jerry Cobb, and I went first to those new tenements near the lumber mill, and then to the Ladds'. Mr. Ladd bought all we had and made us promise to keep the secret until the premium came, and I've been going about ever since then as if the banquet lamp was inside of me all lighted up and burning, for everybody to see."

Rebecca's hair was loosened and falling over her forehead in ruffled waves; her eyes were brilliant, her cheeks crimson; there was a hint of everything in the girl's face—of sensitiveness and delicacy as well as of ardor; there was the sweetness of the mayflower and the strength of the young oak, but one could easily divine that she was one of "The souls by nature pitched too high, By suffering plunged too low."

"That's just the way you look, for all the world as if you did have a lamp burning inside of you," sighed aunt Jane. "Rebecca! I wish you could take things easier, child— I am fearful for you sometimes."

# The Robin who Showed the Way

From *The Secret Garden*
by Frances Hodgson Burnett

I have said before, she was not a child who had been trained to ask permission or consult her elders about things. All she thought about the key was that if it was the key to the closed garden, and she could find out where the door was, she could perhaps open it and see what was inside, and what had happened to the old rose-trees. It was because it had been shut up so long that she wanted to see it. Besides that, if she liked it she could go into it every day and shut the door behind her, and could make up some play of her own and play it alone, because nobody would know where she was, but would think the door was still locked and the key buried in the earth. The thought pleased her very much.

Living as it were, all by herself in a house with a hundred mysteriously closed rooms and having nothing whatever to do to amuse herself, had set her inactive brain to working and was actually awakening her imagination. There is no doubt that the fresh, strong, pure air from the moor had a great deal to do with it. In India she had always been too hot and languid and weak to care much about anything, but in this place she was beginning to care and to want to do new things. Already she felt less "contrary," though she did not know why.

She put the key in her pocket and walked up and down her walk. No one but herself ever seemed to

come there, so she could walk
slowly and look at the wall, or
rather, at the ivy growing on it.
The ivy was the baffling thing.
However carefully she looked
she could see nothing but thickly
growing, glossy, dark green leaves.
She was very disappointed.
Something of her contrariness
came back to her as she paced the
walk and looked over it at the treetops inside. It seemed so silly, she
said to herself, to be near it and not
be able to get in. She took the key
in her pocket when she went back to the house, and
she made up her mind that she would always carry
it with her when she went out, so that if she ever
should find the hidden door she would be ready.

Mrs. Medlock had allowed Martha to sleep all
night at the cottage, but she was back at her work in

the morning with cheeks redder than ever and in the best of spirits.

"I got up at four o'clock," she said. "Eh! it was pretty on th' moor with th' birds gettin' up an' th' rabbits scamperin' about an' th' sun risin'. I didn't walk all th' way. A man gave me a ride in his cart an' I did enjoy myself."

She was full of stories of the delights of her day out. Her mother had been glad to see her and they had got all the baking and washing done. She had even made each of the children a doughcake with a bit of brown sugar in it.

"I had 'em all pipin' hot when they came in from playin' on th' moor. An' th' cottage all smelled o' nice, clean hot bakin' an' there was a good fire, an' they just shouted for joy. Our Dickon he said our cottage was good enough for a king."

In the evening they had all sat around the fire, and Martha and her mother had sewed patches on torn clothes and mended stockings and Martha had told them about the little girl who had come from India and who had been waited on all her life until she didn't know how to put on her own stockings.

"Eh! they did like to hear about you," said Martha. "They wanted to know all about th' people you knew an' about th' ship you came in. I couldn't tell 'em enough."

Mary reflected a little. "I'll tell you a great deal more before your next day out," she said, "so that you will have more to talk about. I dare say they would like to hear about riding on elephants and camels, and about the officers going to hunt tigers."

"My word!" cried delighted Martha. "It would set 'em off their heads. It would be same as a wild beast show like we heard they had in York once."

"India is quite different from Yorkshire," Mary said slowly, as she thought the matter over. "I never thought of that. Did Dickon and your mother like to hear you talk about me?"

"Why, our Dickon's eyes nearly started out o' his

head," answered Martha. "But mother, she was put out about your seemin' to be all by yourself like. She said, "Hasn't Mr. Craven got no governess for her?" and I said, "No, he hasn't, though Mrs. Medlock says he will when he thinks of it, but he mayn't think of it for two or three years.""

"I don't want a governess," said Mary sharply.

"But mother says you ought to be learnin' by this time an' you ought to have a woman to look after you, an' she says: "Now, Martha, think how you'd feel yourself, in a big place like that, wanderin' about all alone, an' no mother. You do your best to cheer her up," she says, an' I said I would."

Mary gave her a long, steady look. "You do cheer me up," she said. "I like to hear you talk."

Presently Martha went out of the room and came back with something held in her hands under her apron. "What does tha' think," she said, with a cheerful grin. "I've brought thee a present."

"A present!" exclaimed Mistress Mary. How

could a cottage full of fourteen hungry people give anyone a present?

"A man was drivin' across the moor peddlin'," Martha explained. "An' he stopped his cart at our door. He had pots an' pans an' odds an' ends, but mother had no money to buy anythin'. Just as he was goin' away our 'Lizabeth Ellen called out, "Mother, he's got skippin'-ropes with red an' blue handles." An' mother she calls out quite sudden, "Here, stop, mister! How much are they?" An' he says, "Tuppence," an' mother she began fumblin' in her pocket an' she says to me, "Martha, tha's brought me thy wages like a good lass, an' I've got four places to put every penny, but I'm just goin' to take tuppence out of it to buy that child a skippin'-rope," an' she bought one an' here it is."

She brought it out from under her apron and exhibited it quite proudly. It was a strong, slender rope with a striped red and blue handle at each end, but Mary Lennox had never seen a skipping-rope before. She gazed at it with a mystified expression.

"What is it for?" she asked curiously.

"For!" cried out Martha. "Does tha' mean that they've not got skippin'-ropes in India, for all they've got elephants and tigers and camels! This is what it's for; just watch me."

And she ran into the middle of the room and, taking a handle in each hand, began to skip, while Mary turned in her chair to stare at her, and the queer faces in the old portraits seemed to stare at her too, and wonder what on earth this common little cottager had the impudence to be doing under their very noses. But Martha did not even see them. The interest and curiosity in Mistress Mary's face delighted her, and she went on skipping and counted out loud as she skipped until she had reached a hundred.

"I could skip longer than that," she said when she stopped. "I've skipped as much as five hundred in one go when I was twelve, but I wasn't as fat then as I am now, an' I was in practice."

Mary got up from her chair beginning to feel excited herself. "It looks nice," she said. "Your mother is a kind woman. Do you think I could ever skip like that?"

"You just try it," urged Martha, handing her the skipping- rope. "You can't skip a hundred at first, but if you practice you'll mount up. Mother she says, "Nothin' will do her more good than skippin' rope. It's th' sensiblest toy a child can have. Let her play out in th' fresh air skippin' an' it'll stretch her legs an' arms an' give her some strength in 'em.""

It was plain that there was not a great deal of strength in Mistress Mary's arms and legs when she first began to skip. She was not very clever at it, but she liked it so much that she did not want to stop.

"Put on tha' things and run an' skip out o' doors," said Martha. "Mother said I must tell you to keep out o' doors as much as you could, even when it rains a bit, so as tha' wrap up warm."

Mary put on her coat and hat and took her skipping-rope over her arm. She opened the door to go out, and then suddenly thought of something and turned back rather slowly.

"Martha," she said, "they were your wages. It was your two-pence really. Thank you." She said it stiffly because she was not used to thanking people or noticing that they did things for her. "Thank you," she said, and held out her hand because she did not know what else to do.

Martha gave her hand a clumsy little shake, as if she was not accustomed to this sort of thing either. Then she laughed. "Run off an' play with thy rope."

Mistress Mary felt a little awkward as she went out of the room.

Yorkshire people seemed strange, and Martha was always rather a puzzle to her. At first she had disliked her very much, but now she did not.

The skipping-rope was a wonderful thing. She counted and skipped, and skipped and counted, until her cheeks were quite red, and she was more interested than she had ever been since she was born. The sun was shining and a little wind was blowing—not a rough wind, but one which came in delightful little gusts and brought a fresh scent of newly turned earth with it.

She skipped around the fountain garden, and up one walk and down another. She skipped at last into the kitchen-garden and saw Ben Weatherstaff digging and talking to his robin, which was hopping about him. She skipped down the walk toward him and he lifted his head and looked at her with a curious expression. She had wondered if he would notice her. She wanted him to see her skip.

"Well!" he exclaimed. "Upon my word. P'raps

tha' art a young 'un, after all, an' p'raps tha's got child's blood in thy veins instead of sour buttermilk. Tha's skipped red into thy cheeks. I wouldn't have believed tha' could do it."

"I never skipped before," Mary said. "I'm just beginning. I can only go up to twenty."

"Tha' keep on," said Ben. "Just see how he's watchin' thee," jerking his head toward the robin. "He followed after thee yesterday. He'll be at it again today. He'll be bound to find out what th' skippin'-rope is. He's never seen one."

Mary skipped around all the gardens and around the orchard, resting every few minutes. At length she went to her own special walk and made up her mind to see if she could skip the whole length of it. It was a good long skip and she began slowly, but before she had gone half-way down the path she was so hot and breathless that she was obliged to stop. She did not mind much, because she had already counted up to thirty. She stopped with a little laugh of pleasure, and there, lo and behold, was the robin swaying on a long branch of ivy. He had followed her and he greeted her with a chirp. As Mary had skipped her way along she had felt something heavy in her pocket strike against her at each jump, and now that she saw the robin she laughed again.

"You showed me where the key was yesterday," she said. "You ought to show me the door today, but I don't believe you know!"

The robin flew from his swinging spray of ivy on to the top of the wall and he opened his beak and sang a loud, lovely trill, merely to show off. Nothing in the world is quite as adorably lovely as a robin when he shows off—and they are nearly always doing it.

Mary Lennox had heard a great deal about magic in her Ayah's stories, and she always said that what happened almost at that moment was magic. One of the nice little gusts of wind rushed down the walk, and it was a stronger one than the rest. It was strong enough to wave the branches of the trees, and it was more than strong enough to sway the trailing sprays of untrimmed ivy hanging from the wall. Mary had stepped close to the robin, and suddenly the gust of wind swung aside some loose ivy trails, and more suddenly still she jumped toward it and caught it in her hand. This she did because she had seen something under it—a round knob that had been covered by the leaves hanging over it. It was the knob of a door.

She put her hands under the leaves and began to pull and push them aside. Thick as the ivy hung, it nearly all was a loose and swinging curtain, though some had crept over wood and iron. Mary's heart began to thump and her hands to shake a little in her delight and excitement. The robin kept singing and twittering away and tilting his head on one side, as if he were as excited as she was. What was this under her hands which was square and made of iron and which her fingers found a hole in?

It was the lock of the door that had been closed ten years and she put her hand in her pocket, drew out the key, and found it fitted the keyhole. She put the key in and turned it. It took two hands to do it, but it did turn. And then she took a long breath and looked behind her up the long walk to see if anyone was coming. No one ever did come, it seemed, and she took another long breath, because she could not help it, and she held back the swinging curtain of ivy and pushed back the door that opened slowly.

Then she slipped through it, and shut it behind her, and stood with her back against it, looking about her and breathing quite fast with excitement, wonder, and delight.

She was standing inside the secret garden.

# SAVING THE DAY

# A Stormy Day

From *Black Beauty*
by Anna Sewell

One day late in the fall my master had a long journey to go on business. I was put into the dogcart, and John went with his master. I always liked to go in the dogcart, it was so light and the high wheels ran along so pleasantly. There had been a great deal of rain, and now the wind was very high and blew the dry leaves across the road in a shower. We went along merrily till we came to the toll-bar and the low wooden bridge. The river banks were rather high, and the bridge, instead of rising, went across just level, so that in the middle, if the river was full, the water would be nearly up to the woodwork, but as there were good substantial rails on each side, people did not mind it.

The man at the gate said the river was rising fast, and he feared it would be a bad night. In one low part of the road the water was halfway up to my knees. The bottom was good, and master drove gently, so it was no matter.

When we got to the town of course I had a good bait, but as the master's business engaged him a long time we did not start for home till late in the afternoon. The wind was then much higher, and I heard the master say to John that he had never been out in such a storm. And so I thought, as we went along the skirts of a wood, where the great branches were swaying about like twigs, and the rushing sound was terrible.

"I wish we were well out of this wood," said my master in a low voice.

"Yes, sir," said John, "it would be rather awkward if one of these branches came down upon us."

The words were scarcely out of his mouth when there was a groan, a crack, and a splitting sound, and tearing, crashing down among the other trees came an oak, torn up by the roots, and it fell right across the road just before us. I will never say I was not frightened, for I was. I stopped still, and I believe I trembled; of course I did not turn round or run away—I was not brought up to that. John jumped out and was in a moment at my head.

"That was a very near touch," said my master. "What's to be done now?"

"Well, sir, we can't drive over that tree, nor yet get around it. There will be nothing for it, but to go back and that will be a good six miles before we get around to the wooden bridge again."

So back we went and around by the crossroads, but by the time we got to the bridge it was very nearly dark; we could just see that the water was over the middle of it; but as that happened sometimes when the floods were out, master did not stop. We were going along at a good pace, but the moment my feet touched the first part of the bridge I felt sure there was something wrong. I dare not go forward, and I made a dead stop. "Go on,

Beauty," said my master, and he gave me a touch with the whip, but I dare not stir. He gave me a sharp cut; I jumped, but I dare not go forward.

"There's something wrong, sir," said John, and he sprang out of the dogcart and came to my head and looked all about. He tried to lead me forward. "Come on, Beauty, what's the matter?" Of course I could not tell him, but I knew very well that the bridge was not safe.

Just then the man at the tollgate on the other side ran out of the house, tossing a torch about like one mad.

"Hoy, hoy, hoy! Halloo! Stop!" he cried.

"What's the matter?" shouted my master.

"The bridge is broken in the middle, and part of it has been carried away; if you come on you'll be into the river."

"Thank God!" said my master.

"You Beauty!" said John, and took the bridle and gently turned me round. The wind seemed to have lulled off after that furious blast which tore up the tree. It grew darker and darker, stiller and stiller. I trotted quietly along, the wheels hardly making a sound on the soft road. For a good while neither master nor John spoke, and then master began in a serious voice. I could not understand much of what they said, but I found they thought, if I had gone on as the master wanted me, most likely the bridge would have given way under us, and horse, chaise, master, and man would have fallen into the river; and as the current was flowing very strongly, it was more than likely we should all have been drowned. Master said, "God had given men reason by which they could find out things for themselves; but he had given animals knowledge that did not depend on reason, and which was much more prompt and perfect in its way, and by which they had often saved the lives of men." John thought people did not value their animals half enough nor make friends of them as they ought to do.

# SAVING THE DAY

At last we came to the park gates and found the gardener looking out for us. He said that mistress had been in a dreadful way ever since dark, fearing some accident had happened, and that she had sent James off on Justice, the roan cob, toward the bridge to inquire after us. As we approached, mistress ran out, saying,

"Have you had an accident?"

"No, my dear; but if your Black Beauty had not been wiser than we were we should all have been carried down the river at the wooden bridge."

Oh, what a good supper he gave me that night—a good bran mash and some crushed beans with my oats, and such a thick bed of straw! And I was glad of it, for I was tired.

# Christmas Wishes

From *Little Women*
by Louisa May Alcott

*The March girls are four sisters. They live with their mother while their father is away from home as Army Chaplain in the Civil War.*

Jo lay on the rug and grumbled, "Christmas won't be Christmas without any presents."

"It's so dreadful to be poor!" sighed Meg, looking down at her old dress.

"I don't think it's fair for some girls to have plenty of pretty things, and other girls nothing at all," added little Amy, with an injured sniff.

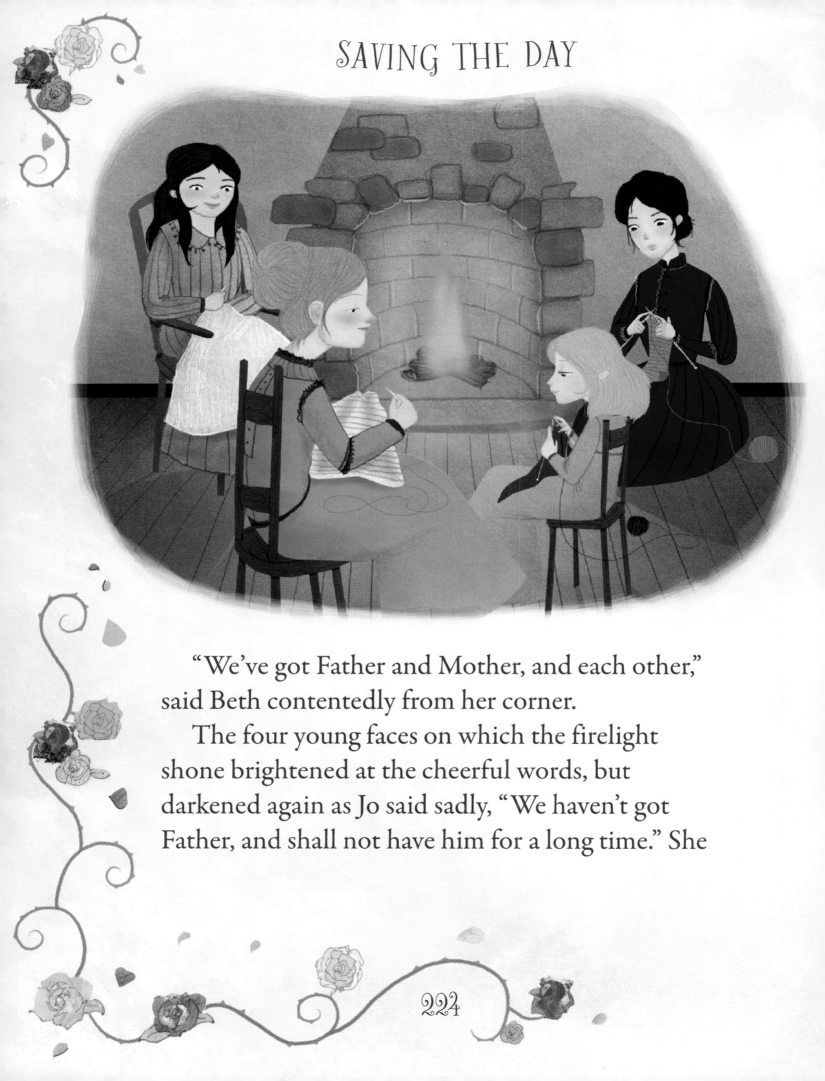

# SAVING THE DAY

"We've got Father and Mother, and each other," said Beth contentedly from her corner.

The four young faces on which the firelight shone brightened at the cheerful words, but darkened again as Jo said sadly, "We haven't got Father, and shall not have him for a long time." She didn't say perhaps never, but each silently added it, thinking of Father far away, where the fighting was.

Nobody spoke for a minute; then Meg said, "You know the reason Mother proposed not having any presents this Christmas was because it is going to be a hard winter for everyone; and she thinks we ought not to spend money for pleasure, when our men are suffering so in the army. We can't do much, but we can make our little sacrifices, and ought to do it gladly. But I am afraid I don't." And Meg shook her head, as she thought regretfully of all the pretty things she wanted.

"But I don't think the little we should spend would do any good. We've each got a dollar, and the army wouldn't be much helped by our giving that. I agree not to expect anything from Mother or you, but I do want to buy *Undine* and *Sintram* for myself. I've wanted it so long", said Jo, who was a bookworm.

"I planned to spend mine in new music," said

Beth, with a little sigh, which no one heard but the hearth brush and kettle holder.

"I shall get a nice box of Faber's drawing pencils. I really need them," said Amy decidedly.

"Mother didn't say anything to us about our money, and she won't wish us to give up everything. Let's each buy something we want, and have a little fun. I'm sure we all work hard enough to earn it," cried Jo, examining the heels of her shoes in a gentlemanly manner.

"I know I do—teaching those tiresome children nearly all day, when I'm longing to enjoy myself at home," began Meg, in the complaining tone again.

"You don't have half such a hard time as I do," said Jo. "How would you like to be shut up for hours with great-aunt March—such a nervous, fussy old lady, who keeps you trotting, is never satisfied, and worries you till you're just about ready to fly out of the window or cry?"

"It's naughty to fret, but I do think washing

dishes and keeping things tidy is the worst work in the world. My hands get so stiff, I can't practice well." And Beth looked at her rough hands with a sigh that anyone could hear that time.

"I don't believe any of you suffer as I do," cried Amy. "For you don't have to go to school with impertinent girls, who plague you if you don't know your lessons, and laugh at your dresses, and label your father if he isn't rich, and insult you when your nose isn't nice."

"If you mean libel, you should say so, and not talk about labels, as if Papa was a pickle bottle," advised Jo, laughing.

"I know what I mean, and you needn't be satirical about it. It's proper to try to use good words, and improve your vocabulary," returned Amy, with dignity.

"Don't peck at one another, children. Don't you wish we had the money Papa lost when we were little, Jo? Dear me! How happy and good we'd be, if we had no worries!" said Meg, who could remember better times.

"You said the other day you thought we were a deal happier than the King children, for they were fighting and fretting all the time, in spite of all their money."

"So I did, Beth. Well, I think we are. For though we do have to work, we make fun of ourselves, and are a pretty jolly set, as Jo would say."

"Jo does use such slang words!" observed Amy, with a reproving look at the long figure stretched on the rug.

Jo immediately sat up, put her hands in her pockets, and began to whistle.

"Don't, Jo. It's so boyish!"

"That's why I do it."

"I detest rude, unladylike girls!"

"I hate affected, niminy-piminy chits!"

"Birds in their little nests agree," sang Beth, the peacemaker, with such a funny face that both sharp voices softened to a laugh, and the pecking ended for that time.

"Really, girls, you are both to be blamed," said Meg, beginning to lecture in her elder-sisterly fashion. "You are old enough to leave off boyish tricks, and to behave better, Josephine. It didn't matter so much when you were a little girl, but now you are so tall, and turn up your hair, you should remember that you are a young lady."

"I'm not! And if turning up my hair makes me one, I'll wear it in two tails till I'm twenty," cried Jo. "I hate to think I've got to grow up, and be Miss March, and wear long gowns, and look as prim as a China Aster! It's bad enough to be a girl, anyway, when I like boy's games and work and manners! I can't get over my disappointment in not being a boy. And it's worse than ever now, for I'm dying to go and fight with Papa. And I can only stay home and knit, like a poky old woman!"

And Jo shook the blue army sock till the needles

rattled like castanets, and her ball bounded across the room.

"Poor Jo! It's too bad, but it can't be helped. So you must try to be contented with making your name boyish, and playing brother to us girls," said Beth, stroking the rough head with a hand that all the dish washing and dusting in the world could not make ungentle in its touch.

"As for you, Amy," continued Meg, "you are altogether too particular and prim. Your airs are funny now, but you'll grow up an affected little goose, if you don't take care. I like your nice manners and refined ways of speaking, when you don't try to be elegant. But your absurd words are as bad as Jo's slang."

"If Jo is a tomboy and Amy a goose, what am I, please?" asked Beth, ready to share the lecture.

"You're a dear, and nothing else", answered Meg warmly, and no one contradicted her, for the "Mouse" was the pet of the family.

As young readers like to know "how people look," we will take this moment to give them a little sketch of the four sisters, who sat knitting away in the twilight, while the December snow fell quietly without, and the fire crackled cheerfully within. It was a comfortable room, though the carpet was faded and the furniture very plain, for a good picture or two hung on the walls, books filled the recesses, chrysanthemums and Christmas roses bloomed in the windows, and a pleasant atmosphere of home peace pervaded it.

Margaret, the eldest of the four, was sixteen, and very pretty, with large eyes, plenty of soft fair hair, a sweet mouth, and white hands, of which she was rather vain.

# SAVING THE DAY

Fifteen-year-old Jo was very tall, thin, and brown, and reminded one of a colt, for she never seemed to know what to do with her long limbs, which were very much in her way. She had a decided mouth, a comical nose, and sharp, gray eyes, which appeared to see everything, and were by turns fierce, funny, or thoughtful. Her long, thick hair was her one beauty, but it was usually bundled into a net, to be out of her way. Round shoulders had Jo, big hands and feet, a fly-away look to her clothes, and the uncomfortable appearance of a girl who was rapidly shooting up into a woman and didn't like it.

Elizabeth, or Beth, as everyone called her, was a rosy, smooth-haired, bright-eyed girl of thirteen, with a shy manner, a soft, timid voice, and a peaceful expression which was seldom disturbed. Her father often called her "Miss Tranquillity," and the name suited her excellently, for she seemed to live in a happy little world of her own, only

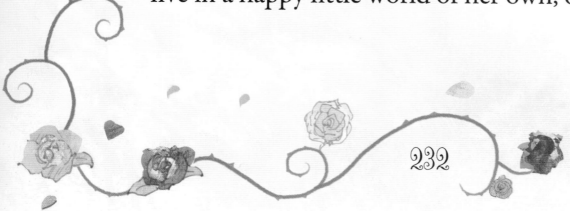

venturing out to meet the few whom she trusted and loved.

Amy, though the youngest, was a most important person, in her own opinion at least. A regular snow maiden, with blue eyes, and yellow hair curling on her shoulders, pale and slender, and always carrying herself like a young lady mindful of her manners. What the characters of the four sisters were we will leave to be found out.

The clock struck six and, having swept up the hearth, Beth put a pair of slippers down to warm. Somehow the sight of the old shoes had a good effect upon the girls, for Mother was coming, and everyone brightened to welcome her. Meg stopped lecturing, and lighted the lamp, Amy drew the easy chair into the best position by the fire, and Jo forgot how tired she was as she sat up to hold the slippers nearer to the blaze.

"They are quite worn out. Marmee must have a new pair."

"I thought I'd get her some with my dollar," said Beth.

"No, I shall!" cried Amy.

"I'm the oldest," began Meg, but Jo cut in with a decided, "I'm the man of the family now Papa is away, and I shall provide the slippers, for he told me to take special care of Mother while he was gone."

"I'll tell you what we'll do," said Beth, "let's each get her something for Christmas, and not get anything for ourselves."

"That's like you, dear! What will we get?" exclaimed Jo.

Everyone thought soberly for a minute, then Meg announced, as if the idea was suggested by the sight of her own pretty hands, "I shall give her a nice pair of gloves."

"Army shoes, best to be had," cried Jo.

"Some handkerchiefs, all hemmed," said Beth.

"I'll get a little bottle of cologne. She likes it, and it won't cost much, so I'll have some left to buy my pencils," added Amy.

"How will we give the things?" asked Meg.

"Put them on the table, and bring her in and see her open the bundles. Don't you remember how we used to do on our birthdays?" answered Jo.

"I used to be so frightened when it was my turn to sit in the chair with the crown on, and see you all come marching around to give the presents, with a kiss. I liked the things and the kisses, but it was dreadful to have you sit looking at me while I opened the bundles," said Beth, who was toasting her face and the bread for tea at the same time.

"Let Marmee think we are getting things for ourselves, and then surprise her. We must go shopping tomorrow afternoon, Meg. There is so much to do about the play for Christmas night," said Jo, marching up and down, with her hands behind her back, and her nose in the air.

"I don't mean to act any more after this time. I'm getting too old for such things," observed Meg.

"You won't stop, I know, as long as you can trail around in a white gown with your hair down, and wear gold-paper jewelry. You are the best actress we've got, and there'll be an end of everything if you quit the boards," said Jo. "We ought to rehearse tonight. Come here, Amy, and do the fainting scene, for you are as stiff as a poker in that."

"I can't help it. I never saw anyone faint, and I don't choose to make myself all black and blue, tumbling flat as you do. If I can go down easily, I'll drop. If I can't, I shall fall into a chair and be graceful. I don't care if Hugo does come at me with a pistol," returned Amy, who was not gifted with dramatic power, but was chosen because she was small enough to be borne out shrieking by the villain of the piece.

"Do it this way. Clasp your hands so, and stagger across the room, crying frantically, 'Roderigo Save me! Save me!'" and away went Jo, with a melodramatic scream that was truly thrilling.

Amy followed, but she poked her hands out stiffly before her, and jerked herself along as if she went by machinery, and her "Ow!" was more suggestive of pins being run into her than of fear and anguish. Jo gave a despairing groan, and Meg laughed outright, while Beth let her bread burn as she watched the fun with interest.

"It's no use! Do the best you can when the time comes, and if the audience laughs, don't blame me. Come on, Meg."

Then things went smoothly, for Don Pedro defied the world in a speech of two pages without a single break. Hagar, the witch, chanted an awful incantation over her kettleful of simmering toads, with weird effect. Roderigo rent his chains asunder manfully, and Hugo died in agonies of remorse and arsenic, with a wild, "Ha! Ha!"

"It's the best we've had yet", said Meg, as the dead villain sat up and rubbed his elbows.

"I don't see how you can write and act such splendid things, Jo. You're a regular Shakespeare!" exclaimed Beth, who firmly believed that her sisters were gifted with wonderful genius in all things.

"Not quite," replied Jo modestly. "I do think *The Witches Curse, an Operatic Tragedy* is rather a nice thing, but I'd like to try *MacBeth*, if we only had a trapdoor for Banquo. I always wanted to do the killing part. "Is that a dagger that I see before me?"" muttered Jo, rolling her eyes, and clutching at the air, as she had seen a famous tragedian do.

"No, it's the toasting fork, with Mother's shoe on it instead of the bread. Beth's stage-struck!" cried Meg, and the rehearsal ended in a burst of laughter.

"Glad to find you so merry, my girls," said a cheery voice at the door, and actors and audience turned to welcome a tall, motherly lady with a "can

# Christmas Wishes

I help you" look about her which was truly delightful. She was not elegantly dressed, but a noble-looking woman, and the girls thought the plain cloak and unfashionable bonnet covered the most splendid mother in the world.

"Well, dearies, how have you got on today? There was so much to do, getting the boxes ready to go tomorrow, that I didn't come home to dinner. Has anyone called, Beth? How is your cold, Meg? Jo, you look tired to death. Come and kiss me, baby."

While making these maternal inquiries Mrs. March got her wet things off, her warm slippers on, and sitting down in the easy chair, drew

Amy to her lap, preparing to enjoy the happiest hour of her busy day. The girls flew about, trying to make things comfortable. Meg arranged the tea table, Jo brought wood and set chairs, dropping, over-turning, and clattering everything she touched. Beth trotted to and fro between parlor and kitchen, quiet and busy, while Amy gave directions to everyone, as she sat with her hands folded.

As they gathered about the table, Mrs. March said, with a particularly happy face, "I've got a treat for you after supper."

A quick, bright smile went around like a streak of sunshine. Beth clapped her hands, regardless of the biscuit she held, and Jo tossed up her napkin, crying, "A letter! A letter! Three cheers for Father!"

"Yes, a nice long letter. He is well, and thinks he shall get through the cold season better than we feared. He sends loving wishes for Christmas, and an especial message to you girls," said Mrs. March, patting her pocket as if she had got a treasure there.

"Hurry and get done! Don't stop to quirk your little finger and simper over your plate, Amy," cried Jo, choking on her tea and dropping her bread, butter side down, on the carpet in her haste to get at the treat.

Beth ate no more, but crept away to sit in her shadowy corner and brood over the delight to come, till the others were ready.

"I think it was so splendid of Father to go as chaplain when he was too old to be drafted, and not strong enough for a soldier," said Meg warmly.

"Don't I wish I could go as a drummer, a vivan—what's its name? Or a nurse, so I could be near him and help him," exclaimed Jo, with a groan.

"It must be very disagreeable to sleep in a tent, and eat all sorts of bad-tasting things, and drink out of a tin mug," sighed Amy.

"When will he come home, Marmee?" asked Beth, with a little quiver in her voice.

"Not for many months, dear, unless he is sick.

He will do his work faithfully as long as he can, and we won't ask for him back a minute sooner than he can be spared. Now come and hear the letter."

They all drew to the fire, Mother in the big chair with Beth at her feet, Meg and Amy perched on either arm of the chair, and Jo leaning on the back, where no one would see any emotion if the letter should happen to be touching. Very few letters were written in those hard times that were not touching, especially those that fathers sent home. In this one little was said of the hardships endured, the dangers faced, or the homesickness conquered.

It was a cheerful, hopeful letter, full of lively descriptions of camp life, marches, and military news, and only at the end did the writer's heart overflow with fatherly love and longing for the little girls at home:

*Give them all of my dear love and a kiss. Tell them I think of them by day, pray for them by night, and find my best comfort in their affection always. A year*

*seems a very long time to wait before I can see them again, but remind them that while we wait we may all work, so that these hard days need not be wasted. I know they will remember all that I said to them, that they will be loving children to you, will do their duty faithfully, and conquer themselves so beautifully that when I come back to them I may be fonder and prouder than ever of my little women.*

Everybody sniffed when they came to that part. Jo wasn't ashamed of the great tear that dropped off the end of her nose, and Amy hid her face on her mother's shoulder and sobbed, "I am a selfish girl! But I'll truly try to be better, so he mayn't be disappointed in me by-and-by."

"We all will," cried Meg. "I think too much of my looks and hate to work, but won't any more, if I can help it."

"I'll try hard to be what he loves to call me, "a little woman" and not be rough and wild, and I shall try to do my duty here instead of wanting to be somewhere else," said Jo, thinking that keeping her temper at home was a much harder task than facing a rebel or two down South.

Beth said nothing, but quietly wiped away her tears with one of the blue army socks and began to knit at once with all her might, losing no time in doing the duty that lay nearest her, while she resolved in her quiet little soul to be all that Father hoped to find her when the year brought around the happy coming home.

Mrs. March broke the silence that followed Jo's words, by saying, "Do you remember how you used to play Pilgrims' Progress when you were little? Nothing delighted you more than to tie my piece bags on your backs for burdens, give you sticks and rolls of paper, and let you travel through the house from the cellar, which was the City of Destruction, to the housetop, where you had lovely things you could collect to make a Celestial City."

"I liked the place where the bundles fell off and tumbled downstairs," said Meg.

"I don't remember much about it, except that I was afraid of the cellar, and always liked the cake and milk we had up at the top. If I wasn't too old for such things, I'd rather like to play it over again," said Amy, who began to talk of renouncing childish things at the mature age of twelve.

"We never are too old for this, my dear, because it is a play we are playing all the time in one way or another. Our burdens are here, our road is before us, and the longing for goodness and happiness is the guide that leads us through many troubles and mistakes to the peace which is a true Celestial City. Now, my little pilgrims, suppose you begin again, not in play, but in earnest, and see how far on you can get before Father comes home."

"Really, Mother? Where are our bundles?" asked Amy, who was a very literal young lady.

"Each of you told what your burden was just

now, except Beth. I rather think she hasn't got any," said her mother.

"I have. Mine is dishes and dusters, and envying girls with nice pianos, and being afraid of people."

Beth's bundle was so funny that everybody wanted to laugh, but nobody did, for it would have hurt her feelings very much.

"Let us do it," said Meg thoughtfully. It is only another name for trying to be good, and the story may help us."

Then out came the four work baskets, and the needles flew as the girls made sheets for Aunt March. It was uninteresting sewing, but tonight no one grumbled. They adopted Jo's plan of dividing the long seams into four parts, and calling the quarters Europe, Asia, Africa, and America, and in that way got on capitally, especially when they talked about the different countries as they stitched their way through them.

At nine they stopped work, and sang, before

they went to bed. No one but Beth could get much music out of the old piano, but she had a way of softly touching the yellow keys and making a pleasant accompaniment to the simple songs they sang. Meg had a voice like a flute, and she and her mother led the little choir. Amy chirped like a cricket, and Jo wandered through the airs at her own sweet will, always coming out at the wrong place with a croak or a quaver that spoiled the most pensive tune. They had done this from the time they could lisp "Crinkle, crinkle, 'ittle 'tar," and it had become a household custom, for mother was a born singer. The first sound in the morning was her voice as she went about the house singing like a lark, and the last sound at night was the same cheery sound, for the girls never grew too old for that familiar lullaby.

# The Wild Wood

From *The Wind in the Willows*
by Kenneth Grahame

The Mole wanted to make the acquaintance of the Badger. He seemed, by all accounts, to be such an important personage and, though rarely visible, to make his unseen influence felt by everybody about the place. But whenever the Mole mentioned his wish to the Water Rat he always found himself put off. "It's all right," the Rat would say. "Badger'll turn up some day or other—he's always turning up—and then I'll introduce you. The best of fellows! But you must not only take him as you find him, but when you find him."

"Couldn't you ask him here to dinner or something?" said the Mole.

"He wouldn't come," replied the Rat simply. "Badger hates Society, and invitations, and dinner, and all that sort of thing."

"Well, then, supposing we go and call on him?" suggested the Mole.

"Oh, I'm sure he wouldn't like that at all," said the Rat, quite alarmed. "He's so very shy, he'd be sure to be offended. I've never even ventured to call on him at his own home myself, though I know him so well. Besides, we can't. It's quite out of the question, because he lives in the very middle of the Wild Wood."

"Well, supposing he does," said the Mole. "You told me the Wild Wood was all right, you know."

"Oh, I know, I know, so it is," replied the Rat evasively. "But I think we won't go there just now. Not just yet. It's a long way, and he wouldn't be at home at this time of year anyhow, and he'll be coming along some day, if you'll wait quietly."

The Mole had to be content with this. But the Badger never came along, and it was not till summer was long over, and cold and frost kept them much indoors, and the swollen river raced past outside their windows with a speed that mocked at boating of any sort or kind, that he found his thoughts dwelling again on the solitary gray Badger, who lived his own life by himself, in his hole in the middle of the Wild Wood.

In the winter time the Rat slept a great deal, retiring early and rising late. During his short day he sometimes scribbled poetry or did small jobs about the house; and, of course, there were always a stream of animals dropping in for a chat, and consequently a good deal of story-telling and comparing notes on the past summer and all its doings.

There was plenty to talk about on those short winter days when the animals found themselves around the fire; still, the Mole had a good deal of spare time on his hands, and so one afternoon, when the Rat in his armchair before the blaze was alternately dozing and trying over rhymes that wouldn't fit, he formed the resolution to go out by himself and explore the Wild Wood, and perhaps strike up an acquaintance with Mr. Badger.

It was a cold, still afternoon with a hard steely sky overhead, when he slipped out of the warm parlor into the open air. The country lay bare and entirely leafless around him, and he thought that he had never seen so far and so intimately into the insides of things as on that winter day when Nature was deep in her annual slumber and seemed to have kicked the clothes off.

# The Wild Wood

Copses, dells, quarries, and all hidden places, which had been mysterious mines for exploration in leafy summer, now exposed themselves and their secrets pathetically, and seemed to ask him to overlook their shabby poverty for a while, till they could riot in rich masquerade as before, and trick and entice him with the old deceptions. It was pitiful in a way, and yet cheering. He was glad that he liked the country undecorated, and stripped of its finery. He had got down to the bare bones of it, and they were fine and strong and simple. He did not want the warm clover and the play of seeding grasses; the billowy drapery of beech and elm seemed best away; and with great cheerfulness of spirit he pushed on towards the Wild Wood, which lay before him low and threatening, like a black reef in some still southern sea.

There was nothing to alarm him at first entry. Twigs crackled under his feet, logs tripped him, funguses on stumps resembled caricatures, and startled him for the moment by their likeness to something familiar and far away; but that was all fun, and exciting. It led him on, and he penetrated to where the light was less, and trees crouched nearer and nearer, and holes made ugly mouths at him on either side.

Everything was very still now. The dusk advanced on him steadily, rapidly, gathering in behind and before; and the light seemed to be draining away like flood-water.

Then the faces began.

It was over his shoulder, and indistinctly, that he first thought he saw a face, a tiny evil wedge-shaped face, looking out at him from a hole. But when he turned and confronted it, the thing had vanished.

He quickened his pace, telling himself cheerfully not to begin imagining things, or there would be simply no end to it. He passed another hole, and another, and another; and then—yes!—no!—yes! certainly a little narrow face, with hard eyes, had flashed up for an instant from a hole, and was gone. He hesitated— braced himself up for an effort and strode on. Then suddenly, and as if it had been so all the time, every hole, far and near—and there were hundreds of them—seemed to possess its own face, coming and going rapidly, all fixing on him glances of malice and hatred: all hard-eyed and evil and sharp.

If he could only get away from the holes in the banks, he thought, there would be no more faces. He swung off the path and plunged into the untrodden places of the wood.

Then the whistling began.

Very faint and shrill it was, and far behind him, when first he heard it; but somehow it made him hurry forward. Then, still very faint and shrill, it sounded far ahead of him, and made him hesitate and want to go back. As he halted in indecision it broke out on either side, and seemed to be caught up and passed on throughout the whole length of the wood to its farthest limit. They were up and alert and ready, evidently, whoever they were! And he—he was alone, and unarmed, and far from any help; and the night was closing in.

Then the pattering began.

He thought it was only falling leaves at first, so slight and delicate was the sound of it. Then as it grew it took a regular rhythm, and he knew it for nothing else but the pat-pat-pat of little feet still a very long way off. Was it in front or behind? It seemed to be first one, and then the other, then both. It grew and it multiplied, till from every quarter as he listened anxiously, leaning this way and that, it seemed to be closing in on him. As he stood still to hearken, a rabbit came running hard toward him through the trees. He waited, expecting it to slacken pace, or to swerve from him into a different course. It stopped and looked at him, before dashing onward. "Get out of this, you fool, get out!" the Mole heard him mutter as he swung around a stump and disappeared down a friendly burrow.

The pattering increased till it sounded like sudden hail on the dry leaf-carpet spread around him. The whole wood seemed running now, running hard, hunting, chasing, closing in around something or—somebody? In panic, he began to run too, aimlessly, he knew not whither. He ran up against things, he fell over things and into things, he darted under things, and dodged around things.

At last he took refuge in the deep dark hollow of an old beech tree, which offered shelter and concealment—and perhaps even safety, but who could be sure? Anyhow, he was too exhausted to run any further, and could only snuggle down into the dry leaves that had drifted into the hollow and hope he was safe for a time. And as the Mole lay in the dark, panting and trembling, and listened to the whistlings and hootings and patterings outside, he knew it at last, in all its fullness: that dread thing, which other little dwellers in field and hedgerow had encountered here, and known as their darkest moment. It was the thing which the kind Rat had tried in vain to shield him from—the Terror of the Wild Wood!

Meantime the Rat, warm and comfortable, dozed by his fireside. His paper of half-finished verses slipped from his knee, his head fell back, his mouth opened, and he wandered by the verdant banks of dream-rivers. Then a coal slipped, the fire crackled and sent up a spurt of flame, and he woke with a start. Remembering what he had been engaged upon, he reached down to the floor for his verses, pored over them for a minute, and then looked around for the Mole to ask him if he knew a good rhyme for something or other.

But the Mole was not there.

The Rat listened for a time. The house seemed very quiet.

Then he called "Moly!" several times. Receiving no answer, he got up and went out into the hall.

The Mole's cap was missing from its accustomed peg. His goloshes, which always lay by the umbrella-stand, were also gone.

The Rat left the house, and carefully examined the muddy surface of the ground outside, hoping to find the Mole's tracks. There they were, sure enough. The goloshes were new, just bought for the winter, and the pimples on their soles were fresh and sharp. He could see the imprints of them in the mud, running along straight and purposeful, leading direct to the Wild Wood.

The Rat looked very grave, and stood in deep thought for a minute or two. Then he re-entered the house, strapped a belt round his waist, shoved a brace of pistols into it, took up a stout cudgel that stood in a corner of the hall, and set off for the Wild Wood at a smart pace.

It was already getting toward dusk when he reached the first fringe of trees and plunged without hesitation into the wood, looking anxiously on either side for any sign of his friend. Here and there wicked little faces popped out of holes, but vanished immediately at sight of the valoros animal, his pistols, and the great ugly cudgel in his grasp; and the whistling and pattering, which he had heard quite plainly on his first entry, died away and

ceased, and all was very still. He made his
way manfully through the length of the
wood, to its furthest edge; then, forsaking
all paths, he set himself to traverse it,
laboriously working over the whole
ground, and all the time calling out
cheerfully, "Moly, Moly, Moly! Where
are you? It's me—it's old Rat!"
He had patiently hunted
through the wood for an hour
or more, when at last to his
joy he heard a little
answering cry. Guiding himself by
the sound, he made his way
through the gathering darkness
to the foot of an old beech tree,
with a hole in it, and from out
of the hole came a feeble voice,
saying, "Ratty! Is that
really you?"

The Rat crept into the hollow, and there he found the Mole, exhausted and still trembling. "Oh Rat!" he cried, "I've been so frightened, you can't think!"

"Oh, I quite understand," said the Rat soothingly. "You shouldn't really have gone and done it, Mole. I did my best to keep you from it. We river-bankers, we hardly ever come here by ourselves. If we have to come, we come in couples, at least; then we're generally all right. Besides, there are a hundred things one has to know, which we understand all about and you don't, as yet. I mean passwords, and signs, and sayings that have power and effect, and plants you carry in your pocket, and verses you repeat, and dodges and tricks you practice; all simple enough when you know them, but they've got to be known if you're small, or you'll find yourself in trouble. Of course if you were Badger or Otter, it would be quite another matter."

"Surely the brave Mr. Toad wouldn't mind

coming here by himself?" inquired the Mole.

"Old Toad?" said the Rat, laughing heartily. "He wouldn't show his face here alone, not for a whole hatful of golden guineas, Toad wouldn't."

The Mole was greatly cheered by the sound of the Rat's careless laughter, as well as by the sight of his stick and his gleaming pistols, and he stopped shivering and began to feel bolder and more like himself again.

"Now then," said the Rat presently, "we really must pull ourselves together and start for home while there's still a little light left. It will never do to spend the night here. Too cold, for one thing."

"Dear Ratty," said the poor Mole, "I'm dreadfully sorry, but I'm simply dead beat and that's a solid fact. You must let me rest here a while longer, and get my strength back, if I'm to get home at all."

"Oh, all right," said the good-natured Rat, "rest away. It's pretty nearly pitch dark now, anyhow; and there ought to be a bit of a moon later."

So the Mole got well into the dry leaves and stretched himself out, and presently dropped off into sleep, though of a broken and troubled sort; while the Rat covered himself up, too, as best he might, for warmth, and lay patiently waiting, with a pistol in his paw.

When at last the Mole woke up, much refreshed and in his usual spirits, the Rat said, "Now then! I'll just take a look outside and see if everything's quiet, and then we really must be off."

He went to the entrance of their retreat and put his head out. Then the Mole heard him saying quietly to himself, "Hullo! hullo! here is a go!"

"What's up, Ratty?" asked the Mole.

"Snow is up," replied the Rat briefly; "or rather, down. It's snowing hard."

The Mole came and crouched beside him, and, looking out, saw the wood that had been so dreadful to him in quite a changed aspect. Holes, hollows, pitfalls, and other black menaces to the wayfarer were vanishing fast, and a gleaming carpet of fairy was springing up everywhere, that looked too delicate to be trodden upon by rough feet. A fine powder filled the air and caressed the cheek with a tingle in its touch, and the trees showed up in a light that seemed to come from below.

"Well, well, it can't be helped," said the Rat, after pondering. "We must make a start, and take our chance, I suppose. The worst of it is, I don't exactly know where we are. And now this snow makes everything look so very different."

It did indeed. The Mole would not have known that it was the same wood. However, they set out bravely, and took the line that seemed most promising, holding on to each other and pretending with cheerfulness that they recognized an old friend in every fresh tree that grimly and silently greeted them, or saw openings, gaps, or paths with a familiar turn in them, in the monotony of white space and black tree trunks that refused to vary.

# SAVING THE DAY

An hour or two later they sat down on a fallen tree trunk to recover their breath and consider what was to be done. They were aching with fatigue and bruised with tumbles; they had fallen into several holes and got wet through; and the trees were thicker and more like each other than ever. There seemed to be no end to this wood, and no beginning, and no difference in it, and, worst of all, no way out.

"We can't sit here very long," said the Rat. "We shall have to make another push for it, and do something or other. The cold is too awful for anything, and the snow will soon be too deep for us to wade through." He peered about him and considered. "Look here," he went on, "this is what occurs to me. There's a sort of dell down here in front of us, where the ground seems all hilly and humpy and hummocky. We'll make our way down into that, and try and find some sort of shelter, a cave or hole with a dry floor to it, out of the snow and the wind, and there we'll have a good rest before we try again, for we're both of us pretty dead beat. Besides, the snow may leave off, or something may turn up."

So once more they got on their feet, and struggled down into the dell, where they hunted about for a cave or some corner that was dry and a protection from the keen wind and the whirling snow. They were investigating one of the hummocky bits the Rat had spoken of, when suddenly the Mole tripped up and fell forward on his face with a squeal.

"Oh my leg!" he cried. "Oh my poor shin!" and he sat up on the snow and nursed his leg in both his front paws.

"Poor old Mole!" said the Rat kindly. "You don't seem to be having much luck today, do you? Let's have a look at the leg. Yes," he went on, going down on his knees to look, "you've cut your shin, sure enough. Wait till I get at my handkerchief, and I'll tie it up for you."

"I must have tripped over a hidden branch or a stump," said the Mole miserably. "Oh, my!"

"It's a very clean cut," said the Rat, examining it again attentively. "That was never done by a branch. Looks as if it was made by a sharp edge of metal. Funny!" He pondered awhile, and examined the humps and slopes that surrounded them.

"Well, never mind what done it," said the Mole, forgetting his grammar in his pain. "It hurts just the same, whatever done it."

But the Rat, after carefully tying up the leg with his handkerchief, had left him and was busy scraping in the snow. He scratched and shoveled and explored, while the Mole waited impatiently, remarking at intervals, "Oh, come on, Rat!"

Suddenly the Rat cried "Hooray!" and then "Hooray-oo-ray-oo-ray-oo-ray!" and fell to executing a feeble jig in the snow.

"What have you found, Ratty?" asked the Mole,

still nursing his leg.

"Come and see!" said the delighted Rat, as he jigged on.

The Mole hobbled up to the spot and had a good look.

"Well," he said at last, slowly, "I see it right enough. Seen the same sort of thing before, lots of times. A door-scraper! Well, what of it? Why dance jigs around a door-scraper?"

"But don't you see what it means, you—you dull-witted animal?" cried the Rat impatiently.

"Of course I see what it means," replied the Mole. "It simply means that some very careless and forgetful person has left his door-scraper lying about in the middle of the Wild Wood, just where it's sure to trip everybody up. Very thoughtless of him, I call it. When I get home I shall go and complain about it to—to somebody or other, see if I don't!"

"Oh, dear! Oh, dear!" cried the Rat, in despair at

his obtuseness. "Here, stop arguing and come and scrape!" And he set to work again and made the snow fly in all directions around him.

After some further toil his efforts were rewarded, and a very shabby door mat lay exposed to view.

"There, what did I tell you?" exclaimed the Rat in great triumph.

"Absolutely nothing whatever," replied the Mole, with perfect truthfulness. "Well now," he went on, "you seem to have found another piece of domestic litter, and I suppose you're perfectly happy. Better go ahead and dance your jig around that if you've got to, and get it over, and then perhaps we can go on and not waste any more time over garbage-heaps. Can we eat a door mat? Or sleep under a door mat? Or sit on a door mat and sledge home over the snow on it, you exasperating rodent?"

"Do you mean to say," cried the excited Rat, "that this door mat doesn't tell you anything?"

"Really, Rat," said the Mole, quite pettishly, "I think we'd had enough of this folly. Who ever heard of a door mat telling anyone anything? They simply don't do it. They are not that sort at all. Door mats know their place."

"Now look here, you—you thick-headed beast," replied the Rat, really angry, "this must stop. Not another word, but scrape and scratch and dig and hunt round, especially on the sides of the hummocks, if you want to sleep dry and warm tonight, for it's our last chance!"

The Rat attacked a snowbank beside them with

ardor, probing with his cudgel everywhere and then digging with fury; and the Mole scraped busily too, more to oblige the Rat than for any other reason, for his opinion was that his friend was getting light-headed.

Some ten minutes' hard work, and the point of the Rat's cudgel struck something that sounded hollow. He worked till he could get a paw through and feel; then called the Mole to come and help him. Hard at it went the two animals, till at last the result of their labors stood full in view of the astonished and hitherto incredulous Mole.

In the side of what had seemed to be a snow bank stood a solid-looking little door, painted a dark green. An iron bell-pull hung by the side, and below it, on a small brass plate, neatly engraved in square capital letters, they could read by the aid of moonlight:

MR. BADGER.

# Saviors of the Train

From *The Railway Children*
by E. Nesbit

Their mother was so delighted with the cherries they had picked for her that the three children racked their brains to think of some other surprise for her. But all the racking did not bring out any idea more novel than collecting wild strawberries. And this idea occurred to them the very next morning.

They had seen the flowers on the plants in the spring, and they knew where to find wild strawberries. The plants grew all up and along the rocky face of the cliff out of which the mouth of the tunnel opened. There were all sorts of trees there—birches and beeches and baby oaks and hazels—and among them the red strawberries glistened on the ground like rubies in the sun.

The mouth of the tunnel was some way from Three Chimneys, so Mother let them take their lunch with them in a basket. And the basket would do to bring the strawberries back in if they found any. She also lent them her silver watch so that they should not be late home for tea—Peter's Waterbury had taken it into its head not to go since the day when Peter dropped it into the waterbutt. And they started.

When they reached the very the top of the cutting, they leaned over the fence and looked down to where the railway lines lay at the bottom of what, as Phyllis said, looked exactly like a mountain gorge.

"If it wasn't for the railway at the bottom, it

would be as though the foot of man had never been there, wouldn't it?" she said.

The sides of the cutting were of gray stone, very roughly hewn. Indeed the top part of the cutting had been a little natural glen that had been cut deeper to bring it down to the level of the tunnel's mouth. Among the rocks, grass and wild flowers grew, and seeds dropped by birds in the crannies of the stone had taken root and grown into bushes and trees that overhung the cutting. Near the tunnel was a flight of steps leading down to the line—no more than wooden bars roughly fixed into the earth—a very steep, narrow way up and down, more like a ladder than a stair.

"We'd better get down," said Peter; "I'm sure the strawberries would be quite easy to get at from the side of the steps. You remember it was there we picked the cherry blossoms that we put on the rabbit's funeral grave."

So they went along the fence toward the little swing gate that is at the top of these steps. And they were almost at the gate when Bobbie said: "Hush. Stop! What's that?"

"That" was a very odd noise indeed—a soft

noise, but quite plainly to be heard through the sound of the wind in the tree branches, and the hum and whirr of the telegraph wires. It was a sort of rustling, whispering sound. As they listened it stopped, and then it began again.

And this time it did not stop, but it grew louder and more rustling and rumbling. "Look," cried Peter, suddenly; "the tree over there!"

The tree he pointed at was one of those that have rough gray leaves and white flowers. The berries, when they come, are bright scarlet, but if you pick them, they disappoint you by turning black before you get them home. And, as Peter pointed, they all saw that the tree was moving—but not just the way that trees ought to move when the wind blows through them, but all in one piece, as though it were a live creature and were walking down the side of the cutting.

"It's moving!" cried Bobbie. "Oh, look! And so are the others. It's like the woods in Macbeth."

"It's magic," said Phyllis, breathlessly. "I always knew this railway was enchanted."

It really did seem a little like magic. For all the trees for about twenty yards of the opposite bank seemed to be slowly walking down toward the railway line, the tree with the gray leaves bringing up the rear like some old shepherd driving a flock of green sheep.

"What is it? Oh, what is it?" said Phyllis; "it's much too magic for me. I don't like it. We should go home."

But Bobby and Peter clung fast to the rail and watched breathlessly. And Phyllis made no movement toward going home by herself.

The trees moved on and on. Some stones and loose earth fell down and rattled on the railway metals far below.

"It's all coming down," Peter tried to say, but he found there was hardly any voice to say it with.

And, indeed, just as he spoke, the great rock, on

the top of which the walking trees were, all leaned slowly forward. The trees, ceasing to walk, stood still and shivered. Leaning with the rock, they seemed to hesitate a moment, and then rock and trees and grass and bushes, with a rushing sound, slipped right away from the face of the cutting and fell on the line with a blundering crash that could have been heard half a mile off. A cloud of dust rose up.

"Oh," said Peter, in awestruck tones, "isn't it exactly like when coals come in? If there wasn't any roof to the cellar and you could see down."

"Look what a great mound it's made!" said Bobbie.

"Yes, it's all gone right across the down line," said Phyllis.

"That'll take some sweeping up," said Bobbie.

"Yes," said Peter, slowly. He was still leaning on the fence. "Yes," he said again, still more slowly.

Then he stood upright. "The 11.29 hasn't gone

by yet. We must let them know at the station, or there'll be a most frightful accident."

"Let's run," said Bobbie, and began.

But Peter cried, "Come back!" and looked at Mother's watch. He was very prompt and businesslike, and his face looked whiter than they had ever seen it.

"No time," he said; "it's two miles away, and it's past eleven."

"Couldn't we," suggested Phyllis, breathlessly, "couldn't we all climb up a telegraph post and do something to the wires?"

"We don't know how to," said Peter.

"They do it in war," said Phyllis; "I know I've heard of it."

"They only cut them, silly," said Peter, "and that doesn't do any good. And we couldn't cut

280

them even if we got up, and we couldn't get up. If we had anything red, we could get down on the line and wave it."

"But the train wouldn't see us till it got around the corner, and then it could see the mound just as well as us," said Phyllis. "Better, because it's much bigger than us."

"But if we only had something red," Peter repeated, "we could go round the corner and wave to the train."

"We might wave, anyway."

"They'd only think it was just us, as usual. We've waved so often before. Anyway, let's get down."

They got down the steep stairs as quickly as they could. Bobbie was pale and shivering. Peter's face looked thinner than usual. Phyllis was red-faced and damp with anxiety.

"Oh, how hot I am!" she said; "and I thought it was going to be cold. I wish we hadn't put on our—" she stopped short, and then ended in quite a different tone "our flannel petticoats."

Bobbie turned at the bottom of the stairs. "Oh, yes," she cried. "They're red! Let's take them off."

They did, and with the petticoats rolled up under their arms, ran along the railway, skirting the newly fallen mound of stones and rock and earth, and bent, crushed, twisted trees. They ran at their best pace. Peter led, but the girls were not far behind. They reached the corner that hid the mound from the straight line of railway that ran half a mile without curve or corner.

"Now," said Peter, taking hold of the largest flannel petticoat.

"You're not—" Phyllis faltered, "you're not going to tear them?"

"Shut up," said Peter, with brief sternness.

"Oh, yes," said Bobbie, "tear them into little bits if you like. Don't you see, Phil, if we can't stop the train, there'll be a real live accident, with people killed. Oh, horrible! Here, Peter, you'll never tear it through the band!"

She took the red flannel petticoat from him and tore it off an inch from the band. Then she tore the other in the same way.

"There!" said Peter, tearing in his turn. He divided each petticoat into three pieces. "Now, we've got six flags." He looked at the watch again. "And we've got seven minutes left. We must have flag-staffs."

The knives given to boys are, for some odd reason, seldom of the kind of steel that keeps sharp. The young saplings had to be broken off. Two of them came up by the roots. The leaves were stripped from them.

"We must cut holes in the flags, and run the sticks through the holes," said Peter. And the holes were cut. The knife was sharp enough to cut flannel with. Two of the flags were set up in heaps of loose stones between the sleepers of the down line.

Then Phyllis and Bobbie each took a flag, and

stood poised, ready to wave it as soon as the train came in sight.

"I shall have the other two myself," said Peter, "because it was my idea to wave something red."

"They're our petticoats, though," Phyllis was beginning, but Bobbie interrupted:

"Oh, what does it matter who waves what, if we can only save the train?"

Perhaps Peter had not rightly calculated the number of minutes it would take the 11.29 to get from the station to the place where they were, or perhaps the train was late. Anyway, it seemed a very long time that they waited.

Phyllis grew impatient. "I expect the watch is wrong, and the train's gone by," said she.

Peter relaxed the heroic attitude he had chosen to show off his two flags with. And Bobbie began to feel sick with suspense.

It seemed to her that they had been standing there for hours and hours, holding those silly little red flannel flags that no one would ever notice. The train wouldn't care. It would just go rushing by them and tear round the corner and go crashing into that awful mound. And everyone on it would be killed.

Her hands grew very cold and trembled so that she could hardly hold the flag. And then came the distant rumble and hum of the metals, and a puff of white steam showed far away along the stretch of line.

"Stand firm," said Peter, "and wave like mad! When it gets to that big furze bush step back, but go on waving! Don't stand on the line, Bobbie!"

The train came rattling along very, very fast.

"They don't see us! They won't see us! It's all no good!" cried Bobbie.

The two little flags on the line swayed as the nearing train shook and loosened the heaps of loose stones that held them up. One of them slowly leaned over and fell on the line. Bobbie jumped forward and caught it up, and waved it; her hands did not tremble now.

"Keep off the line, you silly cuckoo!" hissed Peter, fiercely.

It seemed that the train came on as fast as ever. It was very near now.

"It's no good," Bobbie said again.

"Stand back!" cried Peter, suddenly, and he dragged Phyllis back by the arm.

But Bobbie cried, "Not yet, not yet!" and waved her two flags right over the line. The front of the engine looked black and enormous. It's voice was loud and harsh.

"Oh, stop, stop, stop!" cried Bobbie. No one heard her. At least Peter and Phyllis didn't, for the oncoming rush of the train covered the sound of her voice with a mountain of sound. But afterward she used to wonder whether the engine itself had not heard her. It seemed almost as though it had, for it slackened swiftly, slackened and stopped, not

twenty yards from the place where Bobbie's two flags waved over the line. She saw the great black engine stop dead, but somehow she could not stop waving the flags.

And when the driver and the fireman had got off the engine and Peter and Phyllis had gone to meet them and pour out their excited tale of the awful mound just round the corner, Bobbie still waved the flags but more and more feebly and jerkily.

When the others turned toward her she was lying across the line with her hands flung forward and still holding tight to the sticks of the little red flannel flags.

The engine-driver picked her up, carried her to the train, and laid her gently on the cushions of a first-class carriage.

"Gone right off in a faint," he said, " Poor little woman. And no wonder. I'll just 'ave a look at this 'ere mound of yours, and then we'll run you back to the station and get her seen to."

It was horrible to see Bobbie lying so white and quiet, with her lips blue, and parted.

"I believe that's what people look like when they're dead," whispered Phyllis.

"Don't!" said Peter, sharply.

They sat by Bobbie on the blue cushions, and the train ran back. Before it reached their station Bobbie had sighed and opened her eyes, and rolled herself over and begun to cry. This cheered the others wonderfully. They had seen her cry before, but they had never seen her faint. They had not known what to do when she was fainting, but now she was only crying they could thump her on the back and tell her not to, just as they always did. And presently, when she stopped crying, they were able to laugh at her for being such a coward as to faint.

When the station was reached, the three were the heroes of an agitated meeting on the platform.

The praises they got for their "prompt action," their "common sense," their "ingenuity," were enough to have turned anybody's head. Phyllis enjoyed herself thoroughly. She had never been a real heroine before, and the feeling was delicious. Peter's ears got very red. Yet he, too, enjoyed himself. Only Bobbie wished fervently that they all wouldn't. She wanted to get away.

"You'll hear from the Company about this, I expect," said the Station Master.

Bobbie wished she might never hear of it again. She pulled at Peter's jacket.

"Oh, come away, come away! I want to go home," she said.

So they went. And as they went Station Master and Porter and guards and driver and fireman and passengers sent up a cheer.

"Oh, listen," cried Phyllis; "that's for us!"

"Yes," said Peter, "I say, I am glad I thought about something red, and waving it."

"How lucky we did put on our red flannel petticoats!" said Phyllis.

Bobbie said nothing. She could think only of the horrible mound, and the trustful train rushing toward it at full speed.

"And it was us that saved them," said Peter.

"How dreadful if they'd all been killed!" said Phyllis, with enjoyment; "Wouldn't it, Bobbie?"

"We never got any strawberries, after all," said Bobbie, faintly.

The others thought her rather heartless.

# MUCH MISCHIEF

# A Mad Tea-party

From *Alice's Adventures in Wonderland*
by Lewis Carroll

There was a table set out under a tree in front of the house, and the March Hare and the Hatter were having tea at it.

A Dormouse was sitting between them, fast asleep, and the other two were using it as a cushion, resting their elbows on it, and talking over its head. "Very uncomfortable for the Dormouse," thought Alice; "only, as it's asleep, I suppose it doesn't mind."

The table was a large one, but the three were all crowded together at one corner of it: "No room!

No room!" they cried when they saw Alice coming.

"There's plenty of room!" said Alice indignantly, and she sat down in a large armchair at one end of the table.

"Have some wine," the March Hare said in an encouraging tone.

Alice looked all around the table, but there was nothing on it to drink but tea. "I don't see any wine," she remarked.

"There isn't any," said the March Hare.

"Then it wasn't very civil of you to offer it," said Alice angrily.

"It wasn't very civil of you to sit down without being invited," said the March Hare.

"I didn't know it was your table," said Alice; "it's laid for a great many more than three."

"Your hair wants cutting," said the Hatter. He had been looking at Alice for some time with great curiosity, and this was his first speech.

"You should learn not to make personal

remarks," Alice said with some severity; "it's rude."

The Hatter opened his eyes very wide on hearing this; but all he said was, "Why is a raven like a writing desk?"

"Come, we shall have some fun now!" thought Alice. "I'm glad they've begun asking riddles."

"I believe I can guess that," she added aloud.

"Do you mean that you believe that you can find out the answer to it?" said the March Hare.

"Exactly so," said Alice.

"Then you should say what you mean," the March Hare went on.

"I do," Alice hastily replied; "at least—at least I mean what I say—that's the same thing, you know."

"Not the same thing a bit!" said the Hatter. "You might just as well say that "I see what I eat" is the same thing as "I eat what I see!""

"You might just as well say," added the March Hare, "that 'I like what I get' is the same thing as 'I get what I like!'"

# A Mad Tea-party

"You might just as well say," added the Dormouse, who seemed to be talking in his sleep, 'that I breathe when I sleep' is the same thing as "I sleep when I breathe!'"

"It is the same thing with you," said the Hatter, and here the conversation dropped, and the party sat silent for a minute, while Alice thought over all she could remember about ravens and writing desks, which wasn't much.

The Hatter was the first to break the silence.

"What day of the month is it?" he said, turning to Alice—he had taken his watch out of his pocket, and was looking at it uneasily, shaking it every now and then, and holding it to his ear.

Alice considered for a while, and then said "The fourth."

"Two days wrong!" sighed the Hatter. "I told you butter wouldn't suit the works!" he added looking angrily at the March Hare.

"It was the best butter," the March Hare meekly replied.

"Yes, but some crumbs must have got in as well," the Hatter grumbled, "you shouldn't have put it in with the bread knife."

The March Hare took the watch and looked at it gloomily. Then he dipped it into his cup of tea, and looked at it again; but he could think of nothing better to say than his first remark, "It was the best butter, you know."

Alice had been looking over his shoulder with some curiosity. "What a funny watch!" she remarked. "It tells the day of the month, and doesn't tell what o'clock it is!"

"Why should it?" muttered the Hatter. "Does

your watch tell you what year it is?"

"Of course not," Alice replied very readily: "but that's because it stays the same year for such a long time together."

"Which is just the case with mine," said the Hatter, triumphantly.

Alice felt dreadfully puzzled. The Hatter's remark seemed to have no sort of meaning in it, and yet it was certainly English.

"I don't quite understand you," she said, as politely as she could.

"The Dormouse is asleep again," said the Hatter, and he poured a little hot tea upon its nose.

The Dormouse shook its head impatiently and said, without opening its eyes, "Of course, of course; just what I was going to remark myself."

"Have you guessed the riddle yet?" the Hatter said, turning to Alice again.

"No, I must give it up," Alice replied. "What's the answer?"

"I haven't the slightest idea," said the Hatter.

"Nor I," said the March Hare.

Alice sighed wearily. "I think you might do something better with the time," she said, "than waste it in asking riddles that have no answers."

"If you knew Time as well as I do," said the Hatter, "you wouldn't talk of wasting it. It's him."

"I don't know what you mean," said Alice.

"Of course you don't!" the Hatter said, tossing his head contemptuously. "I dare say you never even spoke to Time!"

"Perhaps not," Alice cautiously replied: "but I know I have to beat time when I learn music."

"Ah! that accounts for it," said the Hatter. "He won't stand beating. Now, if you only kept on good terms with him, he'd do almost anything you liked with the clock. For instance, suppose it were nine o'clock in the morning, just time to begin lessons: you'd only have to whisper a hint to Time, and around goes the clock in a twinkling! Half past one, time for dinner!"

"I only wish it was," the March Hare said to itself in a whisper.

"That would be grand, certainly," said Alice thoughtfully; "but then I shouldn't be hungry for it, you know."

"Not at first, perhaps," said the Hatter: "but you could keep it to half past one as long as you liked."

"Is that the way you manage?" Alice asked.

The Hatter shook his head mournfully. "Not I!" he replied. "We quarreled last March—just before he went mad, you know," (pointing with his tea spoon at the March Hare) "—it was at the great concert given by the Queen of Hearts, and I had to sing "Twinkle, twinkle, little bat! How I wonder what you're at!" You know the song, perhaps?"

"I've heard something like it," said Alice.

"It goes on, you know," the Hatter continued, "in this way:

"Up above the world you fly, Like a tea tray in

the sky. Twinkle, twinkle—""

Here the Dormouse shook itself, and began singing in its sleep, "Twinkle, twinkle, twinkle, twinkle..." and went on so long that they had to pinch it to make it stop.

"Well, I'd hardly reached the end of the first verse," said the Hatter, "when the Queen jumped up and bawled out, "He's murdering the time! Off with his head!""

"How dreadfully savage!" exclaimed Alice.

"And ever since that," the Hatter went on in a mournful tone, "he won't do a thing I ask! It's always six o'clock now."

A bright idea came into Alice's head. "Is that the reason so many tea things have been put out here?" she asked.

"Yes, that's it," said the Hatter with a sigh: "it's always teatime, and we've no time to wash the things between whiles."

"Then you must keep moving around, I suppose?" said Alice.

"Exactly so," said the Hatter; "as the things get used up."

"But what happens when you come to the beginning again?" Alice ventured to ask.

"Suppose we change the subject," the March Hare interrupted, yawning. "I'm getting tired of this. I vote the young lady tells us a story."

"I'm afraid I don't know one," said Alice, rather alarmed at the proposal.

"Then the Dormouse shall!" they both cried. "Wake up, Dormouse!" And they pinched it on both sides at once.

The Dormouse slowly opened his eyes.

"I wasn't asleep," he said in a hoarse, feeble voice. "I heard every word you fellows were saying."

"Tell us a story!" said the March Hare.

"Yes, please do!" pleaded Alice.

"And be quick about it," added the Hatter, "or you'll be asleep again before it's done."

"Once upon a time there were three little sisters," the Dormouse began in a great hurry; "and their names were Elsie, Lacie, and Tillie; and they lived at the bottom of a well—"

"What did they live on?" said Alice, who always took a great interest in questions of eating and drinking.

"They lived on treacle," said the Dormouse, after thinking a minute or two.

"They couldn't have done that, you know," Alice

gently remarked; "they'd have been ill."

"So they were," said the Dormouse; "very ill."

Alice tried to fancy to herself what such an extraordinary way of living would be like, but it puzzled her too much, so she went on: "But why did they live at the bottom of a well?"

"Take some more tea," the March Hare said to Alice, very earnestly.

"I've had nothing yet," Alice replied in an offended tone, "so I can't take more."

"You mean you can't take less," said the Hatter: "it's very easy to take more than nothing."

"Nobody asked your opinion," said Alice.

"Who's making personal remarks now?" the Hatter asked triumphantly.

Alice did not quite know what to say to this, so she helped herself to some tea and bread and butter, and then turned back to the Dormouse, and repeated her question. "Why did they live at the bottom of a well?"

The Dormouse again took a minute or two to think about it, and then said, "It was a treacle-well."

"There's no such thing!" Alice was beginning very angrily, but the Hatter and the March Hare went "Sh! sh!" and the Dormouse sulkily remarked, "If you can't be civil, you had better finish the story for yourself."

"No, please go on!" Alice said very humbly; "I won't interrupt again. I dare say there may be one."

"One, indeed!" said the Dormouse indignantly. However, he consented to go on. "And so these three little sisters—they were learning to draw, you know—"

"What did they draw?" said Alice, quite forgetting her promise.

"Treacle," said the Dormouse, without considering at all this time.

"I want a clean cup," interrupted the Hatter. "Let's all move one place on."

He moved on as he spoke, and the Dormouse

followed him: the March Hare moved into the Dormouse's place, and Alice rather unwillingly took the place of the March Hare. The Hatter was the only one who got any advantage from the change, and Alice was a good deal worse off than before, as the March Hare had just upset the milk jug into his plate.

Alice did not wish to offend the Dormouse again, so she began again very cautiously: "But I don't think I understand. Where did they draw the treacle from?"

"You can draw water out of a water well," said the Hatter; "so I should think you could draw treacle out of a treacle well—eh, stupid?"

"But they were in the well," Alice said to the Dormouse, not choosing to notice this last remark.

"Well, of course they were," said the Dormouse. "Well in."

This answer so confused poor Alice, that she let the Dormouse go on for some time without interrupting it.

"They were learning to draw," the Dormouse went on, yawning and rubbing its eyes, for it was getting very sleepy; "and they drew all manner of things—everything that begins with an "M"—"

"Why with an "M"?" said Alice.

"Why not?" said the March Hare.

Alice was silent.

The Dormouse had closed its eyes by this time, and was going off into a doze; but, on being pinched by the Hatter, it woke up again with a little shriek, and went on: "—that begins with an "M," such as mousetraps, and the moon, and memory, and muchness—you know you say things are "much of a muchness"—did you ever see such a thing as a drawing of a muchness?"

"Really, now you ask me," said Alice, very much confused, "I don't think—"

"Then you shouldn't talk," said the Hatter.

This piece of rudeness was more than Alice

could bear: she got up in great disgust, and walked off. The Dormouse fell asleep instantly, and neither of the others took the least notice of her going, though she looked back once or twice, half hoping that they would call after her. The last she saw of them, they were trying to put the Dormouse into the teapot.

"At any rate I'll never go there again!" said Alice as she picked her way through the wood. "It's the stupidest tea-party I ever was at in all my life!"

Just as she said this, she noticed that one of the trees had a door leading right into it. "That's very curious!" she thought.

"But everything's curious today. I think I may as well go in at once." So she opened the door and in she went.

Once more she found herself in the long hall in which she had first arrived, and close to the little glass table. "Now, I'll manage better this time," she said to herself, and began by taking the little golden key, and unlocking the door that led into the garden. Then she went to work nibbling at the mushroom (she had kept a piece of it in her pocket) till she was about a foot high: then she walked down the little passage; and then she found herself at last in the beautiful garden, among the bright flowerbeds and the cool fountains.

# Pollyanna and Punishments

From *Pollyanna*
by Eleanor H. Porter

*After the death of her father, Pollyanna comes to live with her sour Aunt Polly who is constantly thwarted in her efforts to discipline Pollyanna, who has a perpetually happy outlook on life and is endlessly optimistic.*

At half-past eight Pollyanna went up to bed. The screens had not yet come, and the close little room was like an oven. With longing eyes Pollyanna looked at the two fast-closed windows, but she did not raise them. She undressed, folded her clothes neatly, said her prayers, blew out her candle, and climbed into bed.

Just how long she lay in sleepless misery, tossing from side to side of the hot little cot, she did not know; but it seemed to her that it must have been hours before she finally slipped out of bed, felt her way across the room, and opened her door.

Out in the main attic, all was velvet blackness save where the moon flung a path of silver halfway across the floor from the east dormer window. With a resolute ignoring of that fearsome darkness to the right and to the left, Pollyanna drew a quick breath and pattered straight into that silvery path, and onto the window.

She had hoped that this window might have a screen, but it did not. Outside, however, there was a wide world of fairylike beauty, and there was, too, she knew, fresh, sweet air that would feel so good to hot cheeks and hands!

As she stepped nearer and peered longingly out,

she saw something else: she saw, only a little way below the window, the wide, flat tin roof of Miss Polly's sun parlor. The sight filled her with longing. If only, now, she were out there!

Fearfully she looked behind her. Back there, somewhere, were her hot little room and her still hotter bed; but between her and them lay a horrid desert of blackness across which one must feel one's way with outstretched, shrinking arms; while before her, out on the sun parlor roof, were the moonlight and the cool, sweet night air.

If only her bed were out there! And she knew folks did sleep out of doors. Joel Hartley at home, who was so sick with the consumption, had to sleep out of doors.

Suddenly Pollyanna remembered that she had seen near this attic window a row of long white bags hanging from nails. Nancy had said that they contained the winter clothing, put away for the summer. A little fearfully now, Pollyanna felt her way to these bags, selected a nice fat soft one (it contained Miss Polly's sealskin coat) for a bed; and a thinner one to be doubled up for a pillow, and still another (which was so thin it seemed almost empty) for a covering. Thus equipped, Pollyanna in high glee pattered to the moonlit window again, raised the sash, stuffed her burden through to the roof below, then let herself down after it, closing the window carefully behind her—Pollyanna had not forgotten those flies with the marvelous feet that carried things.

How deliciously cool it was! Pollyanna quite danced up and down with delight, drawing in long, full breaths of the refreshing air. The tin roof under her feet crackled with little resounding snaps that Pollyanna rather liked. She walked, indeed, two or three times back and forth from end to end—it gave her such a pleasant sensation of airy space after her hot little room; and the roof was so broad and flat that she had no fear of falling off. Finally, with a sigh of content, she curled herself up on the sealskin-coat mattress, arranged one bag for a pillow and the other for a covering, and settled herself to sleep.

"I'm so glad now that the screens didn't come," she murmured, blinking up at the stars; "else I couldn't have had this!"

Downstairs in Miss Polly's room next to the sun parlor, Miss Polly herself was hurrying into dressing gown and slippers, her face white and frightened. A minute before she had been telephoning in a shaking voice to Timothy: "Come up quick! You and your father. Bring your lanterns. Somebody is up on the roof of the sun parlor. He must have climbed up the rose-trellis or somewhere, and of course he can get right into the house through the east window in the attic. I have locked the attic door down here—but hurry, quick!"

Some time later, Pollyanna, just dropping off to sleep, was startled by a lantern flash, and a trio of amazed exclamations. She opened her eyes to find Timothy at the top of a ladder near her, Old Tom just getting through the window, and her aunt peering out at her from behind him.

"Pollyanna, what does this mean?" cried Aunt Polly then.

Pollyanna blinked sleepy eyes and sat up. "Why, Mr. Tom—Aunt Polly!" she stammered. "Don't look so scared! It isn't that I've got the consumption, you know, like Joel Hartley. It's only that I was so hot in there. But I shut the window, Aunt Polly, so the flies couldn't carry those germ-things in."

Timothy disappeared suddenly down the ladder. Old Tom, with almost equal precipitation, handed his lantern to Miss Polly, and followed his son. Miss Polly bit her lip hard until the men were gone; then she said sternly:

"Pollyanna, hand those things to me at once and come in here. Of all the extraordinary children!" she exclaimed a little later, as, with Pollyanna by her side and the lantern in her hand, she turned back into the attic.

To Pollyanna the air was all the more stifling after being in that cool breath of the out of doors, but she did not complain. She only drew a long quivering sigh.

At the top of the stairs Miss Polly jerked out crisply: "For the rest of the night, Pollyanna, you are to sleep in my bed with me. The screens will be here tomorrow, but until then I consider it my duty to keep you where I know where you are."

Pollyanna drew in her breath. "With you? In your bed?" she cried rapturously. "Oh, Aunt Polly, Aunt Polly, how perfectly lovely of you! And when

I've so wanted to sleep in the same room with someone, sometime—someone that belonged to me, you know; not a Ladies' Aider. I've had them. My! I reckon I am glad now those screens didn't come! Wouldn't you be?"

There was no reply. Miss Polly was stalking on ahead. Miss Polly, to tell the truth, was feeling curiously helpless. For the third time since Pollyanna's arrival, Miss Polly had been trying to punish Pollyanna, and for the third time she was being confronted with the amazing fact that her punishment was being taken as some kind of special reward of merit. No wonder Miss Polly was feeling curiously helpless.

# Wool and Water

From *Through the Looking-glass*
by Lewis Carroll

Alice looked at the Queen as her voice rose to a squeak. "Much be-etter! Be-etter! Be-e-e-etter! Be-e-ehh!" The last word ended in a long bleat, so like a sheep that Alice quite started.

She looked at the Queen, who seemed to have suddenly wrapped herself up in wool. Alice rubbed her eyes, and looked again. She couldn't make out what had happened at all. Was she in a shop? And was that really—was it really a sheep that was sitting on the other side of the counter? Rub as she could, she could make nothing more of it. She was in a little dark shop, leaning with her elbows on the counter, and opposite to her was an old sheep, sitting in an armchair knitting, and every now and then leaving off to look at her through a great pair of spectacles.

"What is it you want to buy?" the sheep said at last, looking up for a moment from her knitting.

"I don't quite know yet," Alice said, very gently. "I should like to look all around me first, if I might."

"You may look in front of you, and on both sides, if you like," said the sheep: "but you can't look all around you—unless you've got eyes at the back of your head."

But these, as it happened, Alice had not got, so she contented herself with turning around, looking at the shelves as she came to them.

The shop seemed to be full of all manner of curious things—but the oddest part of it all was, that whenever she looked hard at any shelf, to make

out exactly what it had on it, that particular shelf was always quite empty, though the others around it were crowded as full as they could hold.

"Things flow about so here!" she said at last in a plaintive tone, after she had spent a minute or so vainly pursuing a large bright thing, that looked sometimes like a doll and sometimes like a workbox, and was always in the shelf above the one she was looking at. "And this one is the most provoking of all—but I'll tell you what—" she added, as a sudden thought struck her, "I'll follow it up to the very top shelf of all. It'll puzzle it to go through the ceiling, I expect!"

But even this plan failed: the "thing" went through the ceiling as quietly as possible, as if it were quite used to it.

"Are you a child or a teetotum?" the sheep said, as she took up another pair of needles. "You'll make me giddy soon, if you go on turning around and around like that." She was now working with fourteen pairs at once, and Alice couldn't help looking at her in great astonishment.

"How can she knit with so many?" the puzzled child thought to herself. "She gets more and more like a porcupine every minute!"

"Can you row?" the sheep asked, handing her a pair of knitting-needles as she spoke.

"Yes, a little. But not on land—and not with needles—" Alice was beginning to say, when suddenly the needles turned into oars in her hands, and she found they were in a little boat, gliding along between banks, so there was nothing for it but to do her best.

"Feather!" cried the sheep, as she took up another pair of needles.

This didn't sound like a remark that needed any answer, so Alice said nothing, but pulled away. There was something very queer about the water, she thought, as every now and then the oars got fast in it, and would hardly come out again.

"Feather! Feather!" the sheep cried again, taking more needles. "You'll be catching a crab directly."

"A dear little crab!" thought Alice to herself. "I should like that."

"Didn't you hear me say "Feather?"" the sheep cried angrily, taking up quite a bunch of needles.

"Indeed I did," said Alice: "you've said it very often—and very loud. Please, where are the crabs?"

"In the water, of course!" said the sheep, sticking some of the needles into her hair, as her hands were full. "Feather, I say!"

"Why do you say 'feather' so often?" Alice asked at last, rather vexed. "I'm not a bird!"

"You are," said the sheep: "you're a little goose."

This offended Alice a little, so there was no more conversation for a minute, while the boat glided gently on, sometimes among beds of weeds (which made the oars stick fast in the water, worse than ever), and sometimes under trees, but always with the same tall riverbanks frowning over their heads.

"Oh, please! There are some scented rushes!" Alice cried in a sudden transport of delight. "There really are—and such beauties!"

"You needn't say 'please' to me about 'em" the sheep said, without looking up from her knitting: "I didn't put 'em there, and I'm not going to take 'em away."

"No, but I meant—please, may we wait and pick some?" Alice pleaded. "If you don't mind stopping the boat for a minute."

"How am I to stop it?" said the sheep. "If you leave off rowing, it'll stop of itself."

So the boat was left to drift down the stream as it would, till it glided gently in among the waving rushes. And then the little sleeves were carefully rolled up, and the little arms were plunged in elbow-deep to get the rushes a good long way down before breaking them off—and for a while Alice forgot all about the sheep and the knitting, as she bent over the side of the boat, with just the ends of her tangled hair dipping into the water, while with bright eager eyes she caught at one bunch after another of the darling scented rushes.

"I only hope the boat won't tipple over!" she thought to herself. "Oh, what a lovely one! Only I couldn't quite reach it." And it certainly did seem a little provoking—"almost as if it happened on purpose," she thought—that, though she managed to pick plenty of beautiful rushes as the boat glided by, there was always a more lovely one that she couldn't reach.

"The prettiest are always further!" she said at last, with a sigh at the obstinacy of the rushes in growing so far off, as, with flushed cheeks and dripping hair and hands, she scrambled back into her place, and began to arrange her new-found treasures in the boat.

What did it matter to her that the rushes had begun to fade, and to lose all their scent and beauty, from the very moment that she picked them? Even real scented rushes, you know, last only a very little while—and these, being dream-rushes, melted away almost like snow, as they lay in heaps at her feet—but Alice hardly noticed this, there were so many other curious things to think about.

They hadn't gone much farther before the blade of one of the oars got fast in the water and wouldn't come out again, and the consequence was that the handle of it caught her under the chin, and, in spite of a series of little shrieks of "Oh, oh, oh!" from poor Alice, it swept her off the seat, and down among the rushes.

However, she wasn't hurt,

and was soon up again. The sheep went on with her knitting all the while, as if nothing had happened. "That was a nice crab you caught!" she remarked, as Alice got back into her place, very relieved to find herself still in the boat.

"Was it? I didn't see it," said Alice, peeping cautiously over the side of the boat into the dark water. "I wish it hadn't let go—I should so like to see a little crab to take home with me!" But the sheep only laughed scornfully, and went on with her knitting.

"Are there many crabs here?" said Alice.

"Crabs, and all sorts of things," said the sheep: "plenty of choice, only make up your mind. Now, what do you want to buy?"

"To buy!" Alice echoed in a tone that was half astonished and half frightened—for the boat, and the river, had vanished all in a moment, and she was back again in the little dark shop.

"I should like to buy an egg, please," she said

timidly. "How do you sell them?"

"Fivepence farthing for one—twopence for two," the sheep replied.

"Then two are cheaper than one?" Alice asked, taking out her purse.

"Only you must eat them both, if you buy two," said the sheep.

"Then I'll have one, please," said Alice, as she put the money down on the counter. For she thought to herself, "They mightn't be at all nice, you know."

The sheep took the money, and put it away in a box. Then she said, "I never put things into people's hands—that would never do—you must get it for yourself." And so saying, she went off to the other end of the shop, and set the egg upright on a shelf.

"I wonder why it wouldn't do?" thought Alice, as she groped her way among the tables and chairs, for the shop was very dark toward the end. "The egg seems to get further away the more I walk toward it. Let me see, is this a chair? Why, it's got branches, I declare! How very odd to find trees growing here! And actually here's a little brook! Well, this is the very queerest shop I ever saw!"

So she went on, wondering more and more at every step, as everything turned into a tree the moment she came up to it, and she quite expected the egg to do the same.

# The Little Carrs

From *What Katy Did*
by Susan Coolidge

Katy's name was Katy Carr. She lived in the town of Burnet, which wasn't a very big town, but was growing as fast as it knew how. The house she lived in stood on the edge of town. It was a large square house, white, with green blinds, and had a porch in front over which roses and clematis made a thick bower. Four tall locust trees shaded the gravel path that led to the front gate. On one side of the house was an orchard; on the other side were wood piles and barns, and an ice-house. Behind was a kitchen garden sloping to the south; and behind that a pasture with a brook in it, and butternut trees, and four cows—two red ones, a yellow one with sharp horns tipped with tin, and a dear little white one named Daisy.

There were six of the Carr children—four girls and two boys. Katy, the oldest, was twelve years old; little Phil, the youngest, was four, and the rest fitted in between.

# The Little Carrs

Dr. Carr, their Papa, was a dear, kind, busy man, who was away from home all day, taking care of sick people. The children hadn't any Mamma. She had died when Phil was a baby, four years before my story began. Katy could remember her pretty well; to the rest she was but a sad, sweet name, spoken on Sunday, and at prayer-times, or when Papa was specially gentle and solemn.

In place of this Mamma, whom they recollected so dimly, there was Aunt Izzie, Papa's sister, who came to take care of them when Mamma went away on that long journey, from which, for so many months, the little ones kept hoping she might return. Aunt Izzie was a small woman, sharp-faced and thin, rather old-looking, and very neat and particular about everything. She meant to be kind to the children, but they puzzled her very much, because they were not a bit like she herself had been when she was a child. Aunt Izzie had been a gentle, tidy little thing, who loved to sit as Curly Locks did, sewing long seams in the parlor, and to have her head patted by older people, and be told that she was a good girl; whereas Katy tore her dress every day, hated sewing, and didn't care a button about being called "good," while Clover and Elsie shied off like restless ponies when anyone tried to pat their heads. It was very perplexing to Aunt Izzie, and she found it quite hard to forgive the children for being so "unaccountable," and so little like the boys and girls in Sunday-school memoirs, who were the young people she liked best because they always seemed to behave so well, and who she understood most about.

Then Dr. Carr was another person who worried her. He wished to have the children hardy and bold, and encouraged climbing and rough plays, in spite of the bumps and ragged clothes that resulted. In fact, there was just one half-hour of the day when Aunt Izzie was really satisfied about her charges, and that was the half-hour before breakfast, when she had made a law that they were all to sit in their little chairs and learn the Bible verse for the day. At this time she looked at them with pleased eyes— they were all so spick and span, and had such nicely-brushed jackets and such neatly combed hair. But the moment the bell rang her comfort was over. From that time on, they were what she called "not fit to be seen." The neighbors pitied her very much. They used to count the sixty stiff white pantalette legs hung out to dry every Monday morning, and say to each other what a sight of washing those children made, and what a chore it must be for poor Miss Carr to keep them so nice. But poor Miss Carr didn't think them at all nice; that was the worst of it.

"Clover, go upstairs and wash your hands! Dorry, pick your hat off the floor and hang it on the nail! Not that nail, the third nail from the corner!" These were the kind of things Aunt Izzie was saying all day long. The children minded her pretty well, but they didn't exactly love her, I fear. They called her "Aunt Izzie" always, never "Aunty." Boys and girls will know what that meant.

I want to show you the little Carrs, and I don't know that I could ever have a better chance than one day when five out of the six were perched on top of the ice-house, like chickens on a roost. This ice-house was one of their favorite places. It was only a low roof set over a hole in the ground, and, as it stood in the very middle of the side-yard, it always seemed to the children that the shortest road to every place was to go up one of its slopes and down the other.

They also liked to mount to the ridge-pole, and then, still keeping the sitting position, to let go, and scrape slowly down over the warm shingles to the ground. It was bad for their shoes and trousers, of course; but what of that? Shoes and trousers and clothes generally were Aunt Izzie's affair; theirs was to slide and enjoy themselves.

Clover, next in age to Katy, sat at one end. She was a fair, sweet dumpling of a girl, with thick pigtails of light brown hair, and short-sighted blue eyes, which seemed to hold tears, just ready to fall from under the blue. Really, Clover was the jolliest little thing in the world; but these eyes, and her soft cooing voice, always made people feel like petting her and taking her part.

Once, when she was very small, Clover ran away with Katy's doll, and when Katy pursued, and tried to take it back from her, Clover held fast and would not let go. Dr. Carr, who wasn't attending particularly, heard nothing but the pathetic tone of Clover's voice, as she said: "Me won't! Me want Dolly!" and, without stopping to inquire, he called out sharply, "For shame, Katy! Give your sister her doll at once!" which Katy, much surprised, did; while Clover purred in triumph, like a satisfied kitten. Clover was sunny and sweet-tempered, a little indolent, and very modest about herself, though, in fact, she was particularly clever in all sorts of games, and extremely droll and funny in a quiet way. Everybody loved her, and she loved everybody, especially Katy, whom she looked up to as one of the wisest people in the world.

Pretty little Phil sat at the other end. Elsie, a thin, brown child of eight, with beautiful dark eyes, and crisp, short curls covering the whole of her small head sat in the very middle.

Poor little Elsie was the "odd one" among the Carrs. She didn't seem to belong exactly to either the older or the younger children. The great desire and ambition of her heart was to be allowed to go about with Katy and Clover and Cecy Hall, and to know their secrets and be permitted to put notes into the little post offices they were for ever establishing in all sorts of hidden places. But they didn't want Elsie, and used to tell her to "run away and play with the children," which hurt her feelings very much. When she wouldn't run away, I am sorry to say they ran away from her which, as their legs were longest, it was easy to do. Poor Elsie, left behind, would cry bitter tears and, as she was too proud to play much with Dorry and John, her principal comfort was tracking the older ones about and discovering their mysteries, which were her greatest grievance.

Katy, who had the finest plans in the world for being "heroic" and of use, never saw, as she drifted on her heedless way, that here, in this lonely little sister, was the very chance she wanted for being a comfort to somebody who needed comfort very much. And Elsie's heavy heart went uncheered.

Dorry and Joanna sat on either side of Elsie.

Dorry was six years old; a pale, pudgy boy, with rather a solemn face, and smears of molasses on the sleeve of his jacket. Joanna, whom the children called "John," and "Johnnie," was a square, splendid child, a year younger than Dorry; she had big brave eyes, and a wide rosy mouth, which always looked ready to laugh. These two were great friends, though Dorry seemed like a girl who had got into boy's clothes by mistake, and Johnnie like a boy who, in a fit of fun, had borrowed his sister's frock.

And now, as they all sat there chattering and giggling, the window in the house above opened, a glad shriek was heard, and Katy's head appeared. In her hand she held a heap of stockings, which she waved triumphantly.

"Hurray!" she cried, "all done, and Aunt Izzie says we may go. Are you tired out waiting? I couldn't help it, the holes were so big, and took so long. Hurry up, Clover, and get the things! Cecy and I will be down in a minute."

# The Little Carrs

The children all jumped up gladly at once, and slid down the roof. Clover fetched a couple of baskets from the wood shed. Elsie ran for her kitten. Dorry and John loaded themselves with two great bundles of green boughs. Just as they were ready the side-door banged, and Katy and Cecy Hall came into the yard.

I must tell you about Cecy. She was a great friend of the children's, and lived in the house next door. The yards of the houses were only separated by a green hedge with no gate, so that Cecy spent two-thirds of her time at Dr. Carr's, and was exactly like one of the family. She was a neat, dapper, pink-and-white girl, modest and prim in manner, with light shiny hair, which always kept smooth, and slim hands, which never looked dirty. How different from my poor Katy! Katy's hair was forever in a snarl, her gowns were always catching on nails and "tearing themselves" and—in spite of her age and size—she was as heedless and innocent as a child of six. Katy was the longest girl that was ever seen. What she did to make herself grow so, nobody could tell; but there she was—up above Papa's ear and half a head taller than poor Aunt Izzie. Whenever she stopped to think about her height she became very awkward, and felt as if she were all legs and elbows and angles and joints. Happily, her head was so full of other things—of plans and schemes and fancies of all sorts—that she didn't often take time to remember how tall she was.

She was a dear, loving child, for all her careless habits, and made bushels of good resolutions every week of her life, only unluckily she never kept any of them. She had fits of responsibility about the other children, and longed to set them a good example, but when the chance came she generally forgot to do so.

Katy's days flew like the wind; for when she wasn't studying lessons, or sewing and darning with Aunt Izzie (which she hated extremely) there were always so many delightful schemes rioting in her brains, that all she wished for was ten pairs of hands to carry them out.

These same active brains got her into perpetual scrapes. She was fond of building castles in the air, and dreaming of the time when something she had done would make her famous so that everybody would hear of her and want to know her. I don't think she had made up her mind what this wonderful thing was to be; but while thinking about it she often forgot to learn a lesson, or to lace her boots, and then she had a bad mark, or a scolding from Aunt Izzie. At such times she consoled herself with planning how, by and by, she would be beautiful and beloved, and as amiable as an angel.

A great deal was to happen to Katy before that time came. Her eyes, which were black, were to turn blue; her nose was to lengthen and straighten, and her mouth—quite too large at present to suit the part of a heroine—was to be made over into a sort of rosy button. Meantime, and until these charming changes should take place, Katy forgot her features as much as she could, though still, I think, the person on earth whom she most envied was those ladies on the outsides of the shampoo bottles with the wonderful hair that sweeps the ground.

# Golden Guineas

From *Five Children and It*
by E. Nesbit

*Five children are staying in the country while their parents are away.
They discover a "sand-fairy" (the Psammead), who is brown and hairy
with bat's ears and snail's eyes, and seems to be permanently grumpy.
He grants them daily wishes which are quite often disastrous but
which are fortunately unmade at sunset.*

Anthea woke in the morning from a very real sort of dream, in which she was walking in the Zoological Gardens on a pouring wet day without any umbrella. The animals seemed desperately unhappy because of the rain, and were all growling gloomily. When she awoke, both the growling and the rain went on just the same. The growling was the heavy regular breathing of her sister Jane, who had a slight cold and was still asleep. The rain fell in slow drops onto Anthea's face from the wet corner of a towel which her brother Robert was gently squeezing the water out of, to wake her up, as he now explained.

"Oh, drop it!" she said rather crossly; so he did, for he was not a brutal brother, though very ingenious in apple pie beds, booby traps, original methods of awakening sleeping relatives, and all those other little accomplishments which made home happy.

"I had such a funny dream," Anthea began.

"So did I," said Jane, wakening suddenly and without warning. "I dreamed we found a Sand-fairy in the gravel-pits, and it said it was a Psammead, and we might have a new wish every day, and—"

"But that's what I dreamed," said Robert; "I was just going to tell you—and we had the first wish directly it said so. And I dreamed you girls were donkeys enough to ask for us all to be beautiful as the day, and we jolly well were, and of course it was perfectly beastly."

"But can different people all dream the same thing?" said Anthea, sitting up in bed, "because I dreamed all that as well as about the Zoo and the rain. And Baby didn't know us in my dream, and the servants shut us out of the house because the radiantness of our beauty was such a complete disguise, and—"

The voice of the eldest brother sounded from across the landing. "Come on Robert," it said, "you'll be late for breakfast again—unless you mean to shirk your bath like you did on Tuesday."

"I say, come here a sec," Robert replied. "I didn't shirk it; I had it after brekker in father's dressing-room, because ours was emptied away."

Cyril appeared in the doorway, partially clothed.

"Look here," said Anthea, "we've all had such an odd dream. We've all dreamed that we found a Sand-fairy."

Her voice died away before Cyril's contemptuous glance. "Dream?" he said; "You little sillies, it's true. I tell you it all happened. That's why I'm so keen on being down early. We'll go up there directly after brekker, and have another wish. Only we'll make up our minds, solid, before we go, what it is we want, and no one must ask for anything unless the others agree first. No more peerless beauties for this child, thank you. Not if I know it!"

The other three dressed, with their mouths open. If all that dream about the Sand-fairy was real, this real dressing seemed very like a dream, the girls thought. Jane felt that Cyril was right, but Anthea was not sure, till after they had seen Martha and heard her full and plain reminders about their naughty conduct the day before. Then Anthea was sure. "Because," said she, "servants never dream anything but the things in dream-books, like snakes and oysters and going to a wedding—that means a funeral, and snakes are a false female friend, and oysters are babies."

"Talking of babies," said Cyril, "where's the Lamb got to?"

"Martha's going to take him to Rochester to see her cousins. Mother said she might. She's dressing him now," said Jane, "in his very best coat and hat. Bread and butter, please."

"She seems to like taking him too," said Robert in a tone of wonder.

"Servants do like taking babies to see their relations," Cyril said; "I've noticed it before—

especially in their best things."

"I expect they pretend they're their own babies, and that they're not servants at all, but married to noble dukes of high degree, and they say the babies are the little dukes and duchesses," Jane suggested dreamily, taking more marmalade. "I expect that's what Martha'll say to her cousin. She'll enjoy herself most frightfully."

"She won't enjoy herself most frightfully carrying our infant duke to Rochester," said Robert; "not if she's anything like me, she won't."

"Fancy walking to Rochester with the Lamb on your back! Oh, crikey!" said Cyril in full agreement.

"She's going by carrier," said Jane. "Let's see them off, then we shall have done a polite and kindly act, and we shall be quite sure we've got rid of them for the day."

So they did. Martha wore her Sunday dress of two shades of purple, so tight in the chest that it made her stoop, and her blue hat with the pink cornflowers and white ribbon. She had a yellow-lace collar with a green bow. And the Lamb had indeed his very best cream-colored silk coat and hat. It was a smart party that the carrier's cart picked up at the Cross Roads.

When its white tilt and red wheels had slowly vanished in a swirl of chalkdust, Cyril said: "And now for the Psammead!"

And off they went.

As they went they decided on the wish they would ask for. Although they were all in a great hurry they did not try to climb down the sides of the gravel-pit, but went around by the safe lower road, as if they had been carts. They had made a ring of stones around the place where the Sand-fairy had disappeared, so they easily found the spot again. The sun was burning and bright, and the sky was deep blue and without a cloud. The sand was very hot to touch.

"Suppose it was only a dream, after all," Robert

said as the boys uncovered their spades from the sand-heap where they had buried them and began to dig.

"Suppose you were a sensible chap," said Cyril; "one's quite as likely as the other!"

"Suppose you kept a civil tongue in your head," Robert snapped.

"Suppose we girls take a turn," said Jane, laughing. "You boys seem to be getting very warm."

"Suppose you don't come shoving your silly oar in," said Robert, who was now warm indeed.

"We won't," said Anthea quickly. "Robert dear, don't be so grumpy—we won't say a word, you shall be the one to speak to the Fairy and tell him what we've decided to wish for. You'll say it much better than we shall."

"Suppose you drop being a little humbug," said Robert, but not crossly. "Look out—dig with your hands, now!"

So they did, and presently uncovered the

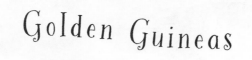

spider-shaped brown hairy body, long arms and legs, bat's ears, and snail's eyes of the Sand-fairy himself. Everyone drew a deep breath of satisfaction, for now of course it couldn't have been a dream. The Psammead sat up and shook the sand out of its fur.

"How's your left whisker this morning?" said Anthea politely.

"Nothing to boast of," said it; "it had rather a restless night. But thank you for asking."

"I say," said Robert, "do you feel up to giving wishes today, because we very much want an extra besides the regular one? The extra's a very little one," he added reassuringly.

"Humph!" said the Sand-fairy. (If you read this story aloud, please pronounce "humph" exactly as it is spelled, for that is how he said it.) "Humph! Do you know, until I heard you being disagreeable to each other just over my head, and so loud too, I really quite thought I had dreamed you all. I do have very odd dreams sometimes."

"Do you?" Jane hurried to say, so as to get away from the subject of disagreeableness. "I wish," she added politely, "you'd tell us about your dreams— they must be awfully interesting."

"Is that the day's wish?" asked the Sand-fairy, yawning and closing its eyes.

Cyril muttered something about "just like a girl," and the rest stood silent. If they said "Yes," then goodbye to the other wishes they had decided to ask for. If they said "No," it would be very rude, and they had all been taught manners, and had learned a little too, which is not at all the same thing. A sigh of relief broke from all lips when the Sand-fairy said: "If I do I shan't have strength to give you a second wish; not even good tempers, or common sense, or manners, or little things like that."

"We don't want you to put yourself out at all about these things, we can manage them quite well ourselves," said Cyril eagerly; while the others looked guiltily at each other, and wished the Fairy would not keep on about good tempers, but give them one good rowing if it wanted to, and then have done with it.

"Well," said the Psammead, putting out his long snail's eyes so suddenly that one of them very nearly went right into Robert's eye, "let's have the little wish first."

"We don't want the servants to notice the gifts you give us."

"Are kind enough to give us," said Anthea in a whisper.

"Are kind enough to give us, I mean," said Robert, hastily.

The Fairy swelled himself out a bit, let his breath go, and said "I've done that for you—it was quite easy. People don't notice things much, anyway. What's the next wish?"

"We want," said Robert slowly, "to be rich beyond the dreams of something or other."

"Avarice," said Jane.

"So it is," said the Fairy unexpectedly. "But it won't do you much good, that's one comfort," it muttered to itself. "Come—I can't go beyond dreams, you know! How much do you want, and will you have it in gold or notes?"

"Gold, please—and millions of it."

"This gravel-pit full be enough?" said the Fairy in an offhand manner.

"Oh yes!"

"Then get out before I begin, or you'll be buried alive in it."

It made its skinny arms so long, and waved them so frighteningly, that the children ran as hard as they could toward the road by which carts used to come to the gravel-pits. Only Anthea had presence of mind enough to shout a timid, "I hope your whisker will be better tomorrow," as she ran.

On the road they turned and looked back, and they had to shut their eyes, and open them very slowly, a little bit at a time, because the sight was too dazzling for their eyes to be able to bear it. It was something like trying to look at the sun at high noon on Midsummer Day. For the whole of the sand-pit was full, right up to the very top, with new shining gold pieces, and all the little sand-martins' little front doors were covered out of sight. Where the road for the carts wound into the gravel-pit the gold lay in heaps like stones lie by the roadside, and a great bank of shining gold shelved down from where it lay flat and smooth between the tall sides of the gravel-pit. And all the gleaming heap was minted gold. And on the sides and edges of these countless coins the midday sun shone and sparkled, and glowed and gleamed till the quarry looked like the mouth of a smelting furnace, or one of the fairy halls that you see sometimes in the sky at sunset.

The children stood with their mouths open, and no one said a word.

At last Robert stooped and picked up one of the loose coins from the edge of the heap by the cart-road, and looked at it. He looked on both sides. Then he said in a low voice, quite different to his own, "It's not sovereigns."

"It's gold, anyway," said Cyril. And now they all began to talk at once. They all picked up the golden treasure by handfuls and let it run through their fingers like water, and the chink it made as it fell was wonderful music. At first they quite forgot to think of spending the money, it was so nice to play with. Jane sat down between two heaps of gold, and Robert began to bury her, as you bury your father in sand when you are at the seaside and he has gone to sleep on the beach with his newspaper over his face.

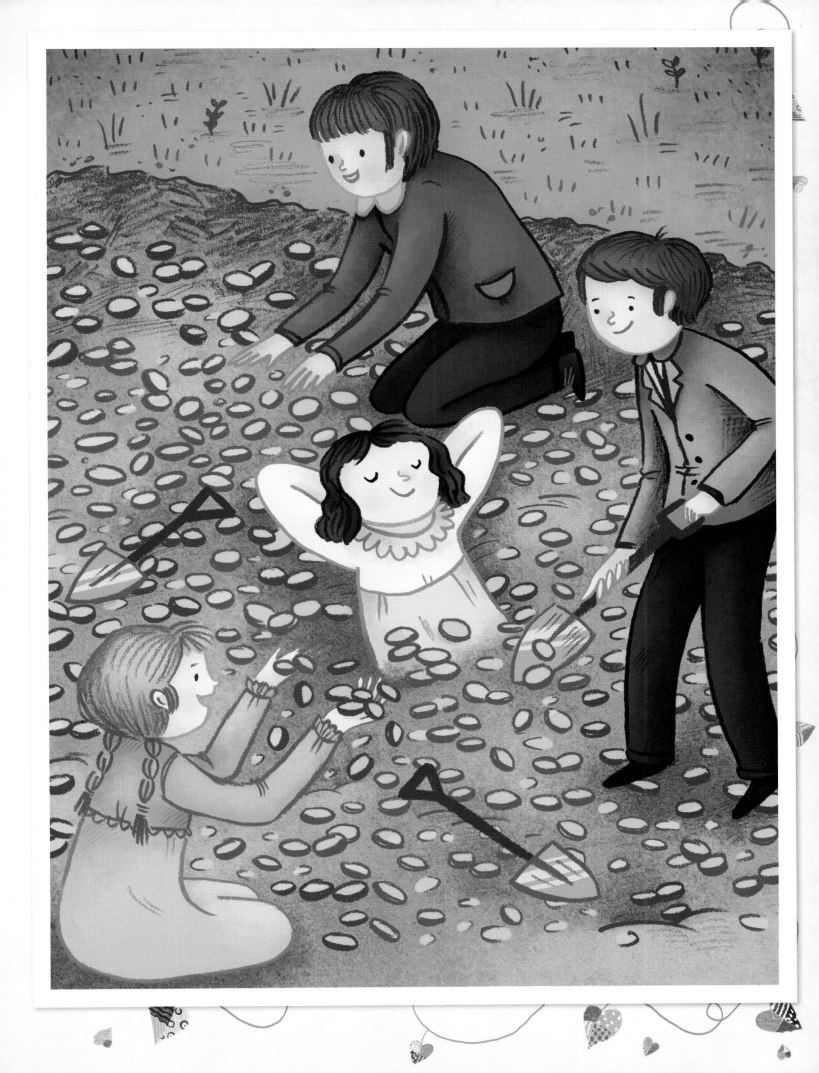

But Jane was not half buried before she cried out, "Oh, stop, it's too heavy! It hurts!"

Robert said "Bosh!" and went on.

"Let me out, I tell you," cried Jane, and was taken out, very white, and trembling a little.

"You've no idea what it's like," she said; "it's like stones on you—or like chains."

"Look here," Cyril said, "if this is to do us any good, it's no good our staying gasping at it like this. Let's fill our pockets and go and buy things. Don't you forget, it won't last after sunset. I wish we'd asked the Psammead why things don't turn to stone. Perhaps this will. I'll tell you what, there's a pony and cart in the village."

"Do you want to buy that?" asked Jane.

"No, silly—we'll hire it. And then we'll go to Rochester and buy heaps and heaps of things. Look here, let's each take as much as we can carry. But it's not sovereigns. They've got a man's head on one side and a thing like the ace of spades on the other.

Fill your pockets with it, I tell you, and come along. You can jaw as we go—if you must jaw."

Cyril sat down and began to fill his pockets. "You all made fun of me for getting father to have nine pockets in my Norfolks," said he, "but now you see!"

They did. For when Cyril had filled his nine pockets and his handkerchief and the space between himself and his shirt front with the gold coins, he had to stand up. But he staggered, and had to sit down again in a hurry.

"Throw out some of the cargo," said Robert. "You'll sink the ship, old chap. That's what comes of nine pockets."

And Cyril had to.

Then they set off to walk to the village. It was more than a mile, and the road was very dusty indeed, and the sun seemed to get hotter and hotter, and the gold coins in their pockets got heavier and heavier.

It was Jane who said, "I don't see how we're to spend it all. There must be thousands of pounds among the lot of us. I'm going to leave some of mine behind this stump in the hedge. And directly we get to the village we'll buy some biscuits—I know it's long past dinnertime." She took out a handful or two of gold and hid it in the hollows of an old hornbeam. "How round and yellow they are," she said. "Don't you wish they were gingerbread nuts and we were going to eat them?"

"Well, they're not, and we're not," said Cyril. "Come on!"

But they came on heavily and wearily. Before they reached the village, more than one stump in the hedge concealed its little hoard of hidden treasure. Yet they reached the village with about twelve hundred guineas in their pockets. But in spite of this inside wealth they looked quite ordinary outside, and no one would have thought they could have more than a half-crown each at the outside. The haze of heat, the blue of the wood smoke, made a sort of dim misty cloud over the red roofs of the village. The four sat down heavily on the first bench they came to. It happened to be outside the Blue Boar Inn.

It was decided that Cyril should go into the Blue Boar and ask for ginger beer, because, as Anthea said, "It is not wrong for men to go into public houses, only for children. And Cyril is nearer to being a man than us, because he is the eldest." So he went. The others sat in the sun and waited.

"Oh, hats, how hot it is!" said Robert. "Dogs put their tongues out when they're hot; I wonder if it would cool us at all to put out ours?"

"We might try," Jane said; and they all put their tongues out as far as they could go, so that it quite stretched their throats, but it only seemed to make them thirstier than ever, besides annoying everyone who went by. So they took their tongues in again, just as Cyril came back with the ginger beer.

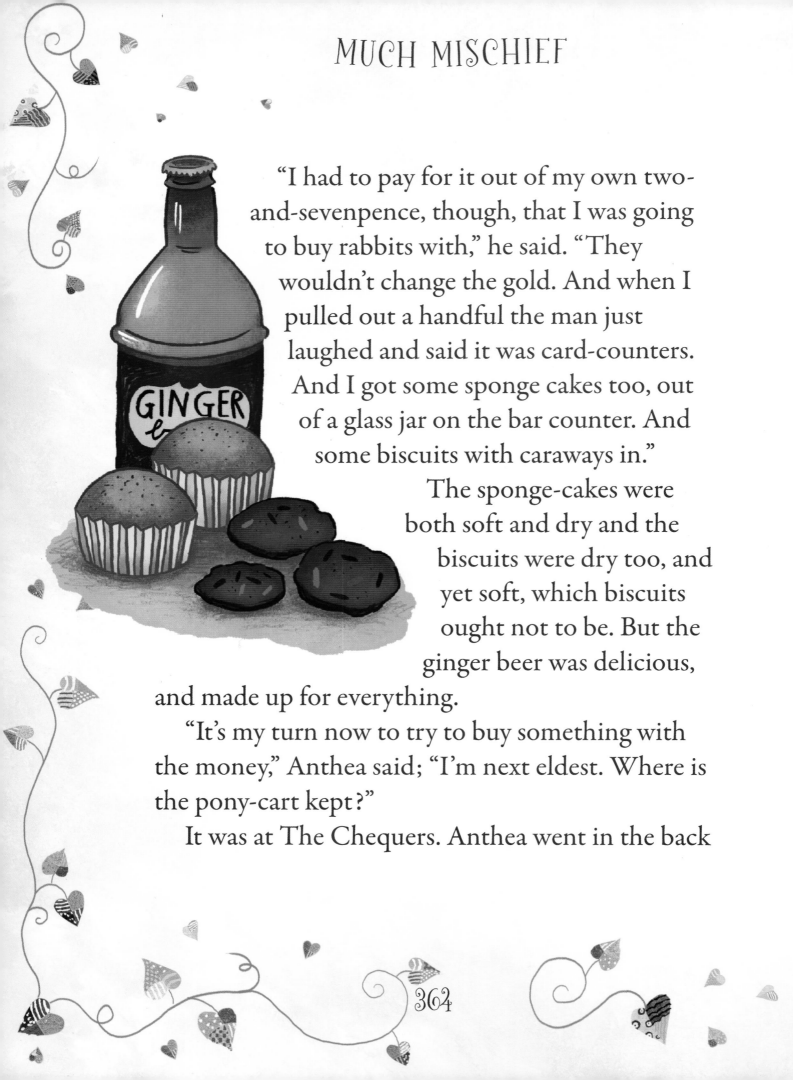

"I had to pay for it out of my own two-and-sevenpence, though, that I was going to buy rabbits with," he said. "They wouldn't change the gold. And when I pulled out a handful the man just laughed and said it was card-counters. And I got some sponge cakes too, out of a glass jar on the bar counter. And some biscuits with caraways in."

The sponge-cakes were both soft and dry and the biscuits were dry too, and yet soft, which biscuits ought not to be. But the ginger beer was delicious, and made up for everything.

"It's my turn now to try to buy something with the money," Anthea said; "I'm next eldest. Where is the pony-cart kept?"

It was at The Chequers. Anthea went in the back

way to the yard, because they all knew that little girls ought not to go into the bars of public houses.

"He'll be ready in a brace of shakes, he says," she remarked, when she came out. "And he's to have one sovereign—or whatever it is—to drive us in to Rochester and back, besides waiting there till we've got everything we want. I think I managed it all quite well."

"You think yourself jolly clever, I daresay," said Cyril moodily. "How did you do it?"

"I wasn't jolly clever enough to go taking handfuls of money out of my pocket, to make it seem cheap, anyway," she retorted.

"I just found a young man doing something to a horse's leg with a sponge and a pail. And I held out one sovereign, and I said, 'Do you know what this is?' He said, 'No,' and he'd call his father. And the old man came, and he said it was a spade guinea; and he said was it my own to do as I liked with, and I said 'Yes'; and I asked about the pony-cart, and I said he could have the guinea if he'd drive us in to Rochester. And his name is S Crispin. And he said, 'Right oh.'"

It was a new sensation to be driven in a smart pony-trap along pretty country roads; it was very pleasant too (which is not always the case with new sensations), quite apart from the beautiful plans of spending the money that each child made as they went along, silently of course and quite to itself, for they felt it would never have done to let the old innkeeper hear them talk in the affluent sort of way they were thinking in. The old man put them down by the bridge at their request.

"If you were going to buy a carriage and horses, where would you go?" asked Cyril, as if he were only asking for the sake of something to say.

"Billy Peasemarsh, at the Saracen's Head," said the old man promptly. "Though all forbid I should recommend any man where it's a question of horses, no more than I'd take anybody else's recommending if I was a-buying one. But if your pa's thinking of a turnout of any sort, there ain't a straighter man in Rochester, nor a civiller spoken, than Billy, though I says it."

"Thank you," said Cyril. "The Saracen's Head."

And now the children began to see one of the laws of nature turn upside down and stand on its head like an acrobat. Any grown-up person would tell you that money is hard to get and easy to spend. But the fairy money had been easy to get, and spending it was not only hard, it was almost impossible. The tradespeople of Rochester seemed to shrink, to a trades person, from the glittering fairy gold ("furrin money" they called it, for the most part).

To begin with, Anthea, who had had the misfortune to sit on her hat earlier in the day, wished to buy another. She chose a very beautiful one, trimmed with pink roses and the blue feathers of peacocks. It was sitting in the window, and was marked, "Paris Model, three guineas."

"I'm glad," she said, "because, if it says guineas, it means guineas, and not sovereigns, which we haven't got."

But when she took three of the spade guineas in her hand, which was by this time rather dirty owing to her not having put on gloves before going to the gravel-pit, the black-silk young lady in the shop looked very hard at her, and went and whispered something to an older and uglier lady, also in black silk, and then they gave her back the money and said it was not current coin.

"But it's good money," said Anthea, "and it is my own."

"I daresay," said the lady, "but it's not the kind of money that's fashionable now, and we don't care about taking it."

"I believe they think we've stolen it," said Anthea, rejoining the others in the street; "if we at least had gloves they wouldn't think we were so dishonest. It's my hands being so dirty that fills their minds with doubts."

So they chose a humble shop, and the girls bought cotton gloves, the kind at sixpence three-farthings, but when they offered a guinea the woman looked at it through her spectacles and said she had no change; so the gloves had to be paid for out of Cyril's two-and-sevenpence that he meant to buy rabbits with, and so had the green imitation crocodile-skin purse at ninepence-halfpenny which had been bought at the same time. They tried several more shops, the kinds where you buy toys and scent, and silk handkerchiefs and books, and fancy boxes of stationery, and photographs of objects of interest in the vicinity.

But nobody cared to change a guinea that day in Rochester, and as they went from shop to shop they got dirtier and dirtier, and their hair got more and more untidy, and Jane slipped and fell down on a part of the road where a water-cart had just gone by.

Also they got very hungry, but they found no one would give them anything to eat for their guineas. After trying the shops of two pastry-cooks in vain, they became so hungry, perhaps from the smell of the cake in the shops, as Cyril suggested, that they formed a plan of campaign in whispers and carried it out in desperation.

They marched into a third pastry cook's—Beale his name was—and before the people behind the counter could interfere each child had seized three new penny buns, clapped the three together between its dirty hands, and taken a big bite out of the triple sandwich. Then they stood at bay, with the twelve buns in their hands and their mouths very full indeed. The shocked pastry cook bounded around the corner.

"Here," said Cyril, speaking as distinctly as he could, and holding out the guinea he got ready before entering the shop, "pay yourself out of that."

Mr. Beale snatched the coin, bit it, and put it into his pocket.

"Off you go," he said, brief and stern like the man in the song.

"But the change?" said Anthea, who had a saving mind.

"Change!" said the man. "I'll change you! Hout you goes; and you may think yourselves lucky I don't send for the police to find out where you got it!"

In the Castle Gardens the millionaires finished the buns, and though the curranty softness of these were delicious, and acted like a charm in raising the spirits of the party, yet even the stoutest heart quailed at the thought of venturing to sound Mr. Billy Peasemarsh at the Saracen's Head on the subject of a horse and carriage. The boys would have given up the idea, but Jane was always a hopeful child, and Anthea generally an obstinate one, and it was their earnestness that prevailed.

The whole party, by this time indescribably dirty, therefore betook itself to the Saracen's Head. The yard-method of attack having been successful at The Chequers was tried again here. Mr. Peasemarsh was in the yard, and Robert opened the business in these terms: "They tell me you have a lot of horses and carriages to sell."

It had been agreed that Robert should be spokesman, because in books it is always the gentlemen who buy horses, and not ladies, and Cyril had had his go at the Blue Boar.

"They tell you true, young man," said Mr Peasemarsh. He was a long, lean man, with very blue eyes and a tight mouth and narrow lips.

"We should like to buy some from you, please," said Robert politely.

"I daresay you would."

"Will you show us a few, please? So that we can all choose?"

"Who are you a-kidden of?" inquired Mr. Billy Peasemarsh. "Was you sent here of a message?"

"I tell you," said Robert, "we want to buy some horses and carriages, and a man told us you were straight and civil spoken, but I shouldn't wonder if he was mistaken."

"Upon my sacred!" said Mr. Peasemarsh. "Shall I trot the whole stable out for your Honor's worship to see? Or shall I send around to the Bishop's to see if he's a nag or two to dispose of?"

"Please do," said Robert, "if it's not too much trouble. It would be very kind of you."

Mr. Peasemarsh put his hands in his pockets and laughed, and they did not like the way he did it. Then he shouted "Willum!"

A stooping ostler appeared in a stable door.

"Here, Willum, come and look at this 'ere young dook! Wants to buy the whole stud, lock, stock, and bar'l. And ain't got tuppence in his pocket to bless hisself with, I'll go bail!"

Willum's eyes followed his master's pointing thumb with contemptuous interest. "Do'e, for sure?" he said.

But Robert spoke, though both the girls were now pulling at his jacket and begging him to "come along." He spoke, and he was very angry; he said: "I'm not a young duke, and I never pretended to be. And as for tuppence—what do you call this?" And before the others could stop him he had pulled out two fat handfuls of shining guineas, and held them out for Mr. Peasemarsh to look at. He did look. He snatched one up in his finger and thumb. He bit it, and Jane expected him to say, "The best horse in my stables is at your service."

But the others knew better. Still it was a blow,

even to the most desponding, when he said shortly: "Willum, shut the yard doors," and Willum grinned and went to shut them.

"Good afternoon," said Robert hastily; "we shan't buy any of your horses now, whatever you say, and I hope it'll be a lesson to you." He had seen a little side gate open, and was moving toward it as he spoke.

But Billy Peasemarsh put himself in the way. "Not so fast, you young off-scouring!" he said. "Willum, fetch the pleece."

Willum went. The children stood huddled together like frightened sheep, and Mr. Peasemarsh spoke to them till the "pleece" arrived. He said many things. Among other things he said: "Nice lot you are, aren't you, coming tempting honest men with your guineas!"

"They are guineas," said Cyril boldly.

"Oh, of course we don't know all about that, no more we don't—oh no—course not! And dragging little gells into it too. 'Ere—I'll let the gells go if you'll come along to the pleece quiet."

"We won't be let go," said Jane heroically; "not without the boys. It's our money just as much as theirs, you wicked old man."

"Where'd you get it, then?" said the man, softening slightly, which was not at all what the boys expected when Jane began to call names.

Jane cast a silent glance of agony at the others.

"Lost your tongue, eh? Got it fast enough when it's for calling names with. Come, speak up. Where'd you get it?"

"Out of the gravel-pit," said truthful Jane.

"Next article," said the man.

"I tell you we did," Jane said. "There's a fairy there—all over brown fur—with ears like a bat's and eyes like a snail's, and he gives you a wish a day, and they all come true."

"Touched in the head, eh?" said the man in a low voice. "All the more shame to you boys dragging the poor afflicted child into your sinful burglaries."

"She's not mad; it's true," said Anthea. "There is a fairy. If I ever see him again I'll wish for something for you; at least I would if vengeance wasn't wicked—so there!"

"Lor' lumme," said Billy Peasemarsh, "if there ain't another on 'em!"

And now Willum came back, with a spiteful grin on his face, and at his back a policeman, with

whom Mr. Peasemarsh spoke long in a hoarse
earnest whisper.

"I daresay you're right," said the policeman at last.
"Anyway, I'll take 'em up on a charge of unlawful
possession, pending inquiries. And the magistrate
will deal with the case. Send the afflicted ones to a
home, as likely as not, and the boys to a
reformatory. Now then, come along, youngsters!
No use making a fuss. You bring the gells along,
Mr. Peasemarsh, sir, and I'll shepherd the boys."

Speechless with rage and horror, the four
children were driven along the streets of Rochester.
Tears of anger and shame blinded them, so that
when Robert ran right into a passer-by he did not
recognize her till a well-known voice said, "Well, if
ever I did. Oh, Master Robert, whatever have you
been a-doing of now?"

And another voice, quite as well known, said,
"Panty; want go own Panty!"

They had run into Martha and the baby!

Martha behaved admirably. She refused to believe a word of the policeman's story, or of Mr. Peasemarsh's either, even when they made Robert turn out his pockets in an archway and show the guineas.

"I don't see nothing," she said. "You've gone out of your senses, you two! There ain't any gold there—only the poor child's hands, all over crock and dirt, and like the very chimbley. Oh, that I should ever see the day!"

And the children thought this very noble of Martha, even if rather wicked, till they remembered how the Fairy had promised that the servants should never notice any of the fairy gifts. So of course Martha couldn't see the gold, and so was only speaking the truth, and that was quite right, of course, but not extra noble.

It was getting dusk when they reached the police station. The policeman told his tale to an inspector, who sat in a large bare room with a thing like a clumsy nursery-fender at one end to put prisoners in. Robert wondered whether it was a cell or a dock.

"Produce the coins, officer," said the inspector.

"Turn out your pockets," said the constable.

Cyril desperately plunged his hands in his pockets, stood still a moment, and then began to laugh—an odd sort of laugh that hurt, and that felt much more like crying. His pockets were empty. So were the pockets of the others. For of course at sunset all the fairy gold had vanished away.

"Turn out your pockets, and stop that noise," said the inspector.

Cyril turned out his pockets, every one of the nine which enriched his Norfolk suit. And every pocket was empty.

"Well!" said the inspector.

"I don't know how they done it—artful little beggars! They walked in front of me the 'ole way, so as for me to keep my eye on them and not to attract a crowd and obstruct the traffic."

"It's very remarkable," said the inspector, frowning.

"If you've quite done a-browbeating of the innocent children," said Martha, "I'll hire a private carriage and we'll drive home to their papa's mansion. You'll hear about this again young man! I told you they hadn't got any gold, when you were pretending to see it in their poor helpless hands. It's early in the day for a constable on duty not to be able to trust his own eyes. As to the other one, the less said the better; he keeps the Saracen's Head, and he knows best what his liquor's like."

"Take them away, for goodness' sake," said the inspector crossly. But as they left the police station he said, "Now then!" to the policeman and Mr. Peasemarsh, and he said it twenty times as crossly as he had spoken to Martha.

Martha was as good as her word. She took them home in a grand carriage, because the carrier's cart was gone, and, though she had stood by them so nobly with the police, she was very angry with them for "trapseing into Rochester," that none of them dared to mention the man with the pony-cart from the village who was still waiting for them. And so, after one day of boundless wealth, the children found themselves sent to bed in disgrace, and only enriched by two pairs of cotton gloves, an imitation crocodile-skin purse, and twelve penny buns, long since digested.

The thing that troubled them most was the fear that the old gentleman's guinea might have disappeared at sunset with all the rest, so they went down to the village next day to apologize for not meeting him in Rochester, and to see. They found him very friendly. The guinea had not disappeared, and he had bored a hole in it and hung it on his watch-chain.

As for the guinea the baker took, the children felt they could not care whether it had vanished or not, which was not perhaps honest, but on the other hand was not unnatural. But afterward this preyed on Anthea's mind, and at last she secretly sent twelve stamps by post to "Mr. Beale, Baker, Rochester." Inside she wrote, "To pay for the buns." I hope the guinea did disappear, for that pastry-cook was really not a nice man and besides, penny buns are seven for sixpence in all respectable shops.

The End